Vision of Hope Infinity #3

By S. Moose

Vision of Hope

Copyright © 2015 S. Moose
Vision of Hope (Infinity #3)

All rights reserved. No part of this publication, may be reproduced,
distributed, or transmitted in any form or by any means, including
photocopying, recording, or other electronic or mechanical methods, without the prior written permission of the publisher.

This is a work of fiction. Names, characters, places and incidents are
the products of the author's imagination or are used fictiously. Any resemblance to actual events, locales, or persons, living or dead, is entirely coincidental.

Editing by
B.Z. Hercules
www.bzhercules.com

Cover Design by
K Keeton Designs
https://www.facebook.com/KKEETONDESIGNS
http://www.kkeetondesigns.com

Photography by
Golden Czermak
https://www.facebook.com/FuriousFotog
http://www.onefuriousfotog.com/

Model
Ryan Patrick
https://www.facebook.com/RyanPatrick0615

Other books by S. Moose

Never Letting Go series
Reaching Out For You
Holding Onto You
Next to Forever

Infinity Series
Vision of Love
Vision of Destiny

Interrupted Series
Interrupted Vol 1
Interrupted Vol 2
Interrupted Vol 3 (Coming soon)

Standalones
Teach Me Love
Beautiful Lessons with Rebecca Brooke

Vision of Hope

Dedication

*To Ryan Patrick.
Thank you for everything.
To the first day we met until now.*

S. Moose

Vision of Hope Playlist

Just a Dream - Carrie Underwood
Be Your Everything - Boys Like Girls
Time of Our Lives - Pitbull
Cry Me a River - Justin Timberlake
On And On - Nick Lachey
Feel Again - One Republic
Angel Eyes - Love and Theft
Buzzkill - Luke Bryan
Crash and Burn - Elise Estrada
Blurred Lines - Robin Thicke
Kiss Me - Ed Sheeran
If You Told Me to - Hunter Hayes
With You - Jessica Simpson
Good to You - Marianas Trench Ft Kate Voegele
Take Your Sweet Time - Jesse McCartney
Love Somebody - Maroon 5
Fall into Me - Brantley Gilbert

Vision of Hope
Table of Contents

Vision of Hope Playlist 5
Prologue 7
Chapter 1 9
Chapter 2 16
Chapter 3 20
Chapter 4 25
Chapter 5 32
Chapter 6 39
Chapter 7 46
Chapter 8 52
Chapter 9 58
Chapter 10 65
Chapter 11 71
Chapter 12 78
Chapter 13 84
Chapter 14 90
Chapter 15 95
Chapter 16 100
Chapter 17 106
Chapter 18 110
Chapter 19 114
Chapter 20 118
Chapter 21 123
Chapter 22 129
Chapter 23 136
Chapter 24 141
Chapter 25 147
Chapter 26 160
Chapter 27 172
Chapter 28 183
Chapter 29 190
Chapter 30 197
Chapter 31 205
Chapter 32 212
Chapter 33 221
Acknowledgements 227
About the Author 229

Prologue

Do you want to hear a story?

It's about a girl who had everything. She was so happy and loved her life. She had an amazing family and a boy who loved her with his whole heart. Then, one day, the girl became lost and wasn't sure what to do. She was scared to leave the one place that held her heart. She asked herself how she could move on and be okay. She looked for signs, but nothing came to her.

Were the signs coming?

Would she know what direction to take?

These were the questions she asked herself. Then, one night, she found herself in her bathroom, staring at a pill bottle. She stared for so long, wondering what would happen if she took the pills.

* * * * *

Putting the bottle to my face, I wonder how fast it would be. My grip around the pill bottle gets stronger. Sobs escape my lungs and slip through my lips. The shattering pain that blisters through pushes me forward. I look at the reflection in the mirror and anger spews from me. Lifting my right arm, I punch the mirror several times, feeling the shards of glass slicing my hand. The pain sears through, but I don't feel it. The pain of my broken heart is stronger.

I grab a piece of the shattered glass and hold it tightly in my hand. I want the pain to go away. I want to feel alive again. I want to breathe, and I want to let go. Since losing him, I've been hiding. No one can pull me out of this. I don't want anyone to. Honestly, I like being alone to think about how I feel without him. When I'm alone, I don't have to pretend to smile to please whoever is around me. Believe me, no one likes to be around suicidal and depressed people. We're the downers, and there's only so much someone can take before they disregard the person.

I'm being disregarded.

Pushing down the top of the bottle, I toss the cap aside and look at the white pills. This is the only way I can be with Brody again.

He's my rock.
My home.
My everything.
Brody.

Chapter 1
Fallyn

"I love you, Fallyn. I..." He closes his eyes, coughing up blood, struggling to talk. "I love you. Always."

"Don't leave me," I sob. "Please don't leave me."

Blood everywhere. Our white sheets soaking in his blood. My clothes and hands covered with his blood. I try to stop the bleeding and grab the sheets to use as band-aids.

"Fallyn, sweetheart, stop."

"No! I have to try! I have to!"

"It's too late. Please stop and look at me." I do as he says. I stare into his hazel eyes. Eyes that I love. Eyes that have saved me so many times. "I'm not going to make it."

"Stop!" I sob, burying my head in his neck. This can't be happening. I'm dreaming and I'm going to wake up in his arms, and we'll be happy and together forever.

"Shhhhh. I want you to promise me that you'll be happy. Live your life and please be happy."

"Not without you. Never without you." My heart shatters into unfixable pieces. The walls around me grow smaller, and I'm falling.

"Brody!" I scream, looking around my dark room and looking to the side. I'm alone in a pool of sweat. The sheets are twisted around my body. I'm gasping for air, closing my eyes, and willing myself to breathe. The raging panic in my chest erupts, leaving me feeling the torment of being alone.

Completely in a daze from my dream, I focus on the reality of my life. I'm here and I'm okay. I'm not back in

Montana. I'm in Wilmington, where I've been for the past six months. I squeeze my eyes shut, willing his body and the blood to leave my mind, and praying that I can go back to sleep.

Breathe. Stop and breathe.

His lifeless body is in my arms. I feel the weight against my body. Covering my eyes with my hands, the familiar numbness of agony plagues me. I scream uncontrollably, grasping the darkness for a rope to pull me out of my mind.

"Fallyn!" My door opens and Isaac runs in. He pulls me into his arms and rocks me back and forth. I sob into his chest, clenching his shirt. "Shhh, it's going to be okay. It's going to be okay."

Exhaustion hits me like a ton of bricks. Exhaustion from crying and dreaming of the past leave my body wrecked and weak. I shiver, needing to find warmth to let out the stress of tonight and welcome sleep. I'm praying that my heart will heal and the tears will soon stop.

If I allow the pain to overtake my body, I'll never be able to see past that night. Willing myself, every day, to move on and live my life how he wants is difficult. How can I live my life when he can't? The absence of his love is strong, and if I let go, then does that mean I don't love him?

I need him to walk through the doors, pull me into his arms, and feel him. I need to feel his arms protecting me, and his kisses making my body swoon and feel like I'm flying. But I know he won't come back.

My breathing slows and soon my eyes close. I feel Isaac putting me down on my bed and pulling the sheets over my body.

"I wish I could take the pain away. I wish you could be happy. Fuck, sis."

I don't want the dreams to go because then he's really gone.

*****

"Good morning, Fallyn!"

"Morning." I smile, taking a gulp of my delicious black coffee. Taking the elevator to the pediatric floor, I lean back against the railing and appreciate this moment of silence. It's been a hectic few weeks and I cannot wait to have tomorrow off.

Moving to Wilmington and accepting a nursing position at New Hanover Regional Medical Center is what I want and I don't regret leaving Montana to be here. I regret the events that happened prior to coming here. Every day is a struggle and I'm trying so hard not to let the weight of reality pull me. Should I have left as soon as I did? Probably not, but Montana stands as a reminder of what could have been.

Life was amazing with him. When I was ten, we met, and I couldn't believe the cute boy in my class was asking me to be his partner. From that day, we became instant best friends. Our parents were friends and we spent day and night together. At sixteen, we became boyfriend and girlfriend. At twenty-one, we got engaged and, at twenty-three, I lost the love of my life.

After his funeral, people frequently came over to send me their condolences, and everywhere I went, I was asked if I was okay. I stood there looking at them and I wasn't sure what to say. *I'm barely living. I think about killing myself so I can be in Heaven with the love of my life. I can't walk by our bedroom because, when I do, I see his bloody body on our bed and the crazy bitch standing by the window, holding a gun to her head.* But I don't say that. I thank them for their condolences.

The scene of that night plays in my head and is permanently on repeat. During the day, it's not too bad, but at night, when I'm alone in the dark, that's when it comes back, reminding me of the hurricane surrounding me. I want the dreams to stop. I want to get through a night without screaming and crying. *Is that too much to ask for?* Nearly everything I love has been ripped away, leaving me with permanent scars and a wall so high around my heart that no one can get through. It's been so long since I've felt a heartbeat with mine. Maybe it's better that way, since it seems as though anyone I love eventually leaves.

The elevator doors open and I make my way to the nursing station. Settling on the chair, taking more sips of my much-needed coffee, I read the notes from the overnight shift.

"Morning, sunshine!"

"Morning, Lexi. How are you?"

"Oh, just peachy." She groans, falling to the chair and tossing her arms in the air in frustration. "Kayden, ugh, kept me up all night and Larry's out of town. I swear, when he's gone, my sweet baby boy turns into the spawn of Satan. He's never this bad when Larry's around."

I burst out laughing, holding my stomach, and setting down my coffee. "You cannot call your son that!"

"Well, why the hell not! He's horrible. But he's with his Aunt Karly now. Hope she can handle both babies. Oh!" She slaps my arm. "When the hell are you coming over and hanging out? We miss you!"

I've known Lexi since starting at the hospital. She was a teacher, but got laid off. After a short time off, she went back to school and got her LPN degree. She's my first friend here and, after a few months, introduced me to her group of friends. Sometimes I wonder if I'm intruding in their lives, but they took in Isaac and me, and I never want to let go.

"Come over next week. We're having a BBQ."

"Next week? Saturday?" I squeak. It's not like I don't want to go out and have fun. I do. Sometimes being a social butterfly is hard, especially seeing my friends with their husbands and families. The ache grows. I think *what if* and wonder if I would be pregnant with Brody's baby if he were still alive.

"Yes." She nods her head. "You work until four that day and you can make it! Don't be a twatwaffle!"

"Did you really just call me that?"

"I did." She sticks out her tongue at me.

Having enough entertainment for this morning, I check on my patients and make sure they're doing okay.

I walk into Eric's room and see he's alone. "Hey, buddy. Where's your mom?"

"She's getting breakfast for us. I hate this hospital food. Seriously, Fallyn, hook me up with something!"

I smile. I love working with the kids. Some of them are here for long stays for treatment and some are here to recover after surgery. Being here on this floor puts things in perspective and, when I'm down and sad, thinking about Brody, I come sit down and talk to the cuties, especially Eric. He's been here for the past six months and the first day I started, I connected with him. A fourteen-year-old boy fighting for his life. He's my little hero.

"How are you holding up today?"

He shrugs. "Okay. Last night was hard. I ran a fever and it hit 102. But I'm okay now. Mom was scared." Eric hangs his head. "I wish my heart would work better. Is that too much to ask for?"

I sit down next to him and take his hand. "You know we're working so hard for you and you're doing so well, Eric. Honey, it's going to be a long road, but, hey, look at you. Look at us. We got this!"

I lift my fist and we bump fists. He laughs and leans back. "You're a dork, Fallyn."

"Only for you, buddy! I'll come back in a few and check up on you. Okay?"

Vision of Hope

"Sounds good."

Walking out of his room, I head back to the nursing station and place my head on the desk.

"Eric?" I groan. "Babe, don't be like that. He's doing a lot better."

"But his fever." I hear Lexi sigh. This is the downfall of being a nurse. We see the good, the bad, and the ugly. Do I hate my job? No. I hate seeing the kids in pain and wondering *why them*? I wish I had the answers to help them understand their circumstances. But instead, I'm here to help them, care for them, and make them live.

"Heads up; Stephen's on his way over."

Stephen Presley. My next-door neighbor. Isaac's bromance. One of the hottest, cockiest, smug bastards I know. He's part of the group of friends Lexi introduced me to, but I met him as soon as we moved in. He's been trying to take me out on a date, but the way his door works, that'll never happen. Each time I look out the kitchen window, I see a new woman doing the walk of shame. He's relentless, but oh-so-fine. If I thought with my lady parts, then I'd be all over him, but I use my head and my heart. And they're still not ready for anything, not even a coffee date.

I can't bring myself to be with another man. The guilt of losing Brody festers and rests in my heart, holding me back from the capability of having a relationship. It makes me nervous, thinking about moving on. I'm still getting used to waking up and not seeing his smiling face staring back at me. Right when I feel like letting go, the thought of moving on comes into my head, and it brings me back to square one. Even though Brody is gone, he's still very much alive in my heart.

"Ladies," Stephen smirks. "Looking sexy as usual."

"Oh, Stephen, why are you here so early in the morning? Need to find a new plaything?" Lexi laughs. "Where's Jensen?"

"With Lisa, duh. You know he's there almost every weekend."

"Damn, she's lucky. Larry's gone so much, and don't get me started on Nicholas. Poor Karly, having to deal with Sebastian *and* Emma. I have Kayden and my little demon spawn is more than enough for me."

"Man, I can't even think about having kids."

"The way you go through women, I'm surprised you don't have little Stephens or Stephanies running around!"

"Hey!" He points at me. "There is *nothing* little about Stephen." He winks and steals my muffin.

"Seriously? You stole my muffin?"

"Mmmm, so good!"

I throw a pen at his head and get up to check on Joey.

Chapter 2
Lisa

We're having a lazy Saturday, staying in bed, cherishing each other, and not caring about the outside world. Right now, in this moment, it's only us.

My eyes slowly open and my gaze turns to Jensen, admiring the slight stubble on his face. His eyes are closed, and his breathing is slow, yet calm. He's dreaming. I smile, lean over, and kiss his cheek. His grip around my body grows tighter. I love being in his arms and feeling safe. Taking the time to really look at him, memorizing his features because tomorrow, he'll be getting on a plane back to Wilmington, while I'll be here in Rochester. So many miles apart, and I'll admit I don't know how I'm going to handle being away from him. Even though we've been together for a year, we spent every day together. Every night, I'd see him and, every morning, I'd wake up in his arms. Three hundred and sixty-five days of pure bliss. How can you be okay with not experiencing that anymore? I'll admit that I'm dependent on Jensen and need him around.

I've been here since the middle of August. At first, it was okay because Jensen would be here with me every weekend, but now that classes are in session, his visits are going to be limited. This is how it has to be. The decision I made to transfer schools wasn't easy. Now that I'm here at Fisher, I'm starting over as a freshman. I didn't realize that the standard of knowledge and learning would be different between the two colleges, but this is what Fisher wants. Finding that out nearly made me want to change my mind and stay in Wilmington. Yet my head was telling me to go.

Before meeting Jensen, I was a player and never truly wanted to settle down. I've never been in love before and never thought that love was for me. All of the emotions since starting our relationship were worth it. It was a little rocky because he dated my best friend Karly, had a baby with Jamie, and kept his heart guarded. It took a while to break down his walls, but once he opened his heart to me, he loved me unconditionally.

Jensen Toscano is an amazing lover and a man with a big heart. When he loves, he loves with his whole heart and shows it with his words and actions. Having Jensen here with me makes things better, but hard. He believes we're going to get through this and I want to believe it too. Long distance relationships are difficult to maintain. My mind yells at me to stop doubting him and us. Then the other irrational part of me says to give him up and take a chance to be alone so I can experience the full being-away-from-home-in-college effect. I know this is selfish of me and I should appreciate Jensen and what he's done for me. I love him, don't get me wrong; it's just hard.

"I love you," I whisper, kissing his sexy back up to his neck. I close my eyes for a few moments, reveling in this quiet moment, remembering the amazing night we shared. I feel his kisses over my body and the way he moved in and out of me. My body tingles for him and screams for more. I'll always want more when it comes to him.

People want perfection and the fairytale without trying or making sacrifices. If Jensen and I didn't have the obstacles, we wouldn't be as strong as we are now.

"Stop thinking," Jensen mutters, turning over and bringing me to his chest. My favorite place.

"I'm not. And how would you know?"

We separate for a moment; our eyes connect. "Because I do. You breathe a little slower and you get sweaty." He laughs. "We're together, Lisa, and that's what matters. We've been doing great since you've been here. Since I met you..." He pauses, stroking my face. "...my life has meaning. You give me reason, Lisa. I was lost and broken, and you found me."

I sigh. "You always know how to make me smile." He leans to kiss my cheek. "I know that we love each other and it'll work out. It's hard, babe. We went from spending every day together to just whenever you can find the time to come see me. I wish you could come every weekend."

"Me too, but you know I can't." He sighs, stroking my arm. "You need to focus on classes and getting your work done. You said it yourself, that Fisher is a lot harder. I'm willing to make these sacrifices so you can have a great future. Your dream is my dream. Whatever you want, I'll work my hardest to give it to you. But if I come here every weekend, then we're not going to appreciate the time we have together. I know it's tough." He cradles my face, giving me a kiss on my forehead, nose, and cheek. "We'll make it through."

"Promise?"

"Promise."

As I wrap my naked body against his, my hand gets curious as I run it down his toned abs. His eyes close as my hand inches closer to his cock. Damn, I love his cock. Stroking it up and down, I kiss his chest and hear him moan. Within seconds, he flips me onto my back and hovers over me, giving me more kisses until his tongue takes over my mouth. The wetness pools between my thighs and I want him.

His fingers brush my shoulder down to my breasts, rubbing my nipples with his fingers. "Oh God," I mutter. His mouth finds each breast, taking his time to suck and nip, causing me to arch my back.

"Shh. I need you to be quiet, baby." He laughs, kissing from my chest to my belly. "You want more?"

"Yes," I moan, raising my hips. That's all he needs to hear before he pushes himself inside me without warning.

"Fuck," he hisses, rocking back and forth. "I love the way you feel around my cock, babe. Fuck so good."

"Keep going," I scream, moaning his name, gripping his strong arms.

He slows down and looks at me. "You are my life," he whispers between soft kisses. "Everything about you is perfect, babe."

I wrap my arms around his neck and bring his lips closer to mine. I've never been good with words; I'm better with actions. Jensen knows how I feel about him without me telling him. Our tongues meet again as I wrap my legs around his waist. He picks me up, still inside me, and settles me on his lap. I love riding his hard cock and the control I have. He makes me feel beautiful and I don't care if my boobs are bouncing or if something jiggles. Jensen doesn't care. He loves me for *me*.

His finger slides down my face, past my nose, and down my neck, sending chills down my body. I pull away from him, bringing his other hand to my lips and I suck on each finger and hear him hiss. His hooded eyes are full of desire and need. I move back a little and guide his hand to my wet pussy as I start fucking him. As I throw my head back, his fingers dominate me.

"Mine." His voice is low and deep. "Always mine."

"Yours."

Chapter 3
Jensen

All I want is to be back in my bed with Lisa and cherish her body all night long. But no, she insisted on leaving the apartment and getting dinner. I guess eating *food* is more important than eating one of my favorite parts of her body. My desire and need for Lisa is on a level even I don't understand sometimes. She's captivated me and pushed herself in my life, taking a permanent stay where I need her to be.

When I first met Lisa, I was in a dark place. Jamie controlled me and made me do things I regret every day. But I did what she wanted for Karly and my daughter, Emma. Lisa saw past all of that and accepted me. I admire her. She fought hard for us when I pushed her away. She's everything I want and makes me want to be a better man. I guess that's what love does to you—it makes you feel like you can conquer the world and, when you fall, you have someone who'll catch you and guide you on the right path.

I glance over to my girl as we're sitting at dinner, enjoying a wine at her new favorite place—Black and Blue. She's beautiful and everything I want. I've never felt like this before, never in my life. My heart squeezes, sitting here and looking at her. I know this is hard for her.

"Are you okay?" she asks me.

"Yeah, babe, no worries. Just thinking." She doesn't respond to my answer and goes on about her classes. I can hear her excitement, but also sadness. I know she misses me and wants me to move here with her. Unfortunately, picking up and leaving, especially leaving Emma, is too difficult. Even though she'll never know me as her dad, I'm her favorite uncle. I'd do anything for my daughter, and this is why I can't ever tell her the truth. In her eyes, Nicholas is her dad and I'm her uncle. That's how it has to be. Sacrifices are made to protect the ones we love. And I love that little girl with my life.

"So you're leaving tomorrow," she pouts.

"Baby, I'll be back in a few weeks," I say, reaching for her hand. "I need you to be the strong woman I know you are. Everything will be okay. I promise."

We spend the rest of the night talking. It's moments like these that I love with her, and it's moments like these I hate because I know it'll be two weeks until I see her again.

Resting on the couch back in her apartment, my fingers twirl her hair as she watches TV. Neither of us has said anything, not knowing what to say. But it's these times when words aren't needed.

When you meet someone special, you feel it in your heart and she's all you think about. No matter how far the distance, if you love someone, you'll make it work. Words can't explain love. It's a feeling that makes life better. We feel wanted and needed and we have the capability to make someone smile. All the obstacles and bullshit that come along the way are worth it when the love is real.

"I wanna show you something," I pull out a picture from my bag on the side of the couch and hand it to her.

She studies the picture, her eyes going wide with surprise, I'm hoping. "Is this what I think it is?" I nod. "You got a house?" I nod again.

"Not just any house." I pause, making sure I find the right words. "A house for us. When you're home from break, I want you with me and, when you're done with school, I want you to move in so we can start our life together. Before you freak out, I'm not asking you to marry me yet." I smile, thinking that spending my life with Lisa feels right. This feels right. "Just a step towards that direction."

The house is near Nicholas and Karly's. The living room holds a stone fireplace and a little nook for Lisa. I think that little spot was the deal breaker. Everything in the house is open and wide. The kitchen's been remodeled with granite and marble, the floor a stone granite. With large bay windows surrounding the house and a balcony in the master bedroom, I know this is the house for Lisa and me.

"I love it," she whispers. She throws her arms around my neck, I pull her against me, feeling her heart beating with mine. "Thank you for doing this for us."

"I would do anything for you, Lisa. You're my world."

I slide my hand up her thigh, placing it on her stomach and tease her lips with mine. Little whimpers leave her lips causing my dick to strain against my jeans. Lying her down on the couch, I push her dress up, sliding her thong off.

"Yes, Jensen," she moans as I kiss her stomach down to her pussy.

Pushing two fingers inside and spreading her wider open I bury my face between her legs. "You fucking taste so good, babe."

"Ahhhhh, keep going."

I flick my tongue against her clit as her legs wrap around my neck. Her body squirms against my lips. "Stop moving, babe," I whisper, holding her down with my other hand. Hands are in my hair and her breathing quickens. She's about to come as I pull away from her, kissing her stomach up to her lips. Grabbing her from the couch, she wraps her legs around my waist. Her lips find my neck and I feel her licking and sucking. Kicking my bedroom door open I throw her against the wall and thrust inside of her. Desperately needing to feel her lips on mine, I gently bite on her lower lip, teasing her, before our tongues meet.

"Lisa. I'll never get enough of you. Every day, every minute with you makes me feel alive." I kiss her lips and cheek, slowing my pace.

"I love you," she whispers against my lips in between our kisses. It's all I need to hear before we both find our release. "I don't want you to go." We sink down on the floor together as I hold her in my arms, breathing her in, never wanting to let go.

"Come on and shower with me before we go to bed," I smirk, hoping to lighten the mood and see her smile.

* * * * *

Holding her in my arms at the airport, I whisper how much I love her and tell her it'll be okay. Looking in her eyes makes me feel whole again. There wasn't anything I wouldn't do to keep her beautiful smile. Right now, it's hard, but it's worth it.

We'll get to see each other at least every other weekend as long as there are no emergencies at the hospital. I've worked it out where I can be gone every other weekend. I'll mostly travel to see her, since her workload is heavy with classes.

"You'll see me in two weeks."

"That's so long, though," she cries. "Why can't you move here?"

"You know I can't," I start responding. "When you're done with school, you'll be back home. We'll make this work, babe. Don't worry, okay?" She nods, pressing her face closer to my chest.

After a few more minutes like this, I let her go and tell her I'll call her when I'm home. Leaving is hard, but I know I'll see her again. We don't need to see each other all the time to make our relationship work. The distance is good and healthy for us. It'll make me miss her and we'll appreciate the time we have together.

Vision of Hope

Lisa has a chance to live and enjoy her college life without me being her shadow. It'll be worth it when she's done with school. Stepping through security, I get situated and wait for my plane to leave.

Life is slowly settling down and I'm able to focus on the important things in my life, like Emma and Lisa.

Boarding the plane, I put in my ear buds and relax for the long flight home.

* * * * *

Monday morning comes too soon. After I park my car in the garage, I send Lisa a text message, wishing her a good day. Picking up my bag and files, I head inside the hospital and go to my office. Sitting down with my mug of coffee and blueberry scone, I review some files. My mind is only on Lisa and my focus is shit.

It's fine that she's not texting me back right away. I look at my clock and notice the time. She's been in class for ten minutes. God, I sound like a crazy stalker. My phone vibrates and, instantly, I'm sliding my finger across the screen to unlock my phone. It's not a text message from Lisa.

Karly: *Lunch?*
Me: *Sure. You bringing =)*
Karly: *Of course. Sushi?*
Me: *Please.*
Karly: *See you at 12!*

Chapter 4
Fallyn

I make my final rounds and stop to see Eric. He's watching TV and his mom, Connie, is on the couch, reading on her Kindle.

"Go take a break," I suggest to her, "I can stay with him for a few minutes."

"Thank you, Fallyn." She gets up and kisses Eric on the cheek, telling him she'll be back.

"Hey, buddy. How are you feeling today?" Grabbing his chart, I take a quick look and smile. "Looks like you've been having a few good days."

He smiles. "I feel so good. I hope to get out soon and play basketball with my friends. Did you know that a girl I like came to visit me last week? Her name's Hannah and she said she'll come to see me more often."

"That's so sweet, Eric!'

"So, do you have a boyfriend?"

Typically, I don't talk about my personal life, especially with my patients, but it's Eric and he's so sweet, I can't resist. "I don't, but that doesn't mean anything. I love being here with everyone."

"Everyone deserves love. No matter where you are in life or how you're doing. I mean, look at me. There are days I don't think I'm going to make it, and then there are days I'm feeling great. Love is weird like that."

Vision of Hope

I laugh so hard. I never would have thought someone as young as Eric would know anything about love. It's inspiring and touching.

"Don't give me that look," he mocks. "My mom's obsessed with reading books, so she sometimes reads aloud and I listen. Chicks dig that kind of stuff."

"I'm sure you're going to be the best boyfriend."

"I hope so."

After talking to Eric and Connie, I head out of the hospital and drive home. All I want is my couch, wine, and TV.

Dropping my purse on the counter, I head to the living room and plop on the couch. It's been a very long sixteen hours at the hospital and I honestly need to unwind. Having a few moments of peace to myself is needed. Some people take moments of silence for granted, but not me. After all the hustle and bustle at the hospital it's nice to be alone and let your mind clear.

"Oh! Wine," I mutter, getting up from the couch. Walking to the kitchen, I open the fridge and pull out a bottle of wine. Pouring myself a healthy glass, I settle back on the couch and turn on the TV. Flipping through the channels, I give up and head to my room. I sit on my bed and stare at a picture of Brody and me that is on the nightstand. It was taken the night he proposed to me.

"Brody, what are you doing?"

"Close your eyes."

I do as he says and feel his hand in mine. "Open them, sweetheart." When I open my eyes, my jaw drops and tears soon fill my eyes. "When I was ten years old, I met this adorable girl. She was so shy and so unsure of herself. I sat next to her and we became best friends. I fell in love with this shy girl and knew I had to have her. But she kept me as her friend, and that was okay for a while. While I dated other girls to get my mind off her, it didn't work. So I stopped dating and waited for her to see that I was standing right in front of her. When we turned sixteen, I knew I had to have her. See, the shy girl was growing up, turning into a beautiful girl, and people noticed. I asked her to be my girlfriend and, to my surprise, she said yes. We fit together and she took my breath away. And now, at twenty-one, I'm kneeling on my one knee, looking at this amazing and beautiful woman who has had my heart for the past eleven years. Fallyn Nicole Phillips, will you grow old with me?"

I smile, touching the picture, savoring the tender moment from that day. "Hi, Brody." I look up at his picture again. We do this a few times a day. "Another shift down. So Eric's doing really good! Part of me is scared that his fever will come back, but I'm going to be strong and believe he's going to make it through. I've been pulling doubles and I'm so exhausted. Sometimes I wonder if I'm making a difference in their lives." I pause, pondering about being a nurse. Then I remember his words. *You're only one person who will touch millions of lives. You'll do your best and never give up. Sometimes, you'll feel defeated and lose a patient, but remember, you are one person who is giving her all to help strangers because she loves, she cares, and she comforts.* "I heard you saying that to me today while I was sitting with Eric." A tear rolls down my face and hits my lap. "I miss you every day." Silence. "I love you, Brody. Always and forever."

I hear the door open and put down the picture. Knowing it's Isaac, I walk out of my bedroom and join him in the kitchen. His back's to me. "Hey!"

"Hi, sis." He turns around and leans against the counter, looking at my glass of wine. "It's five o'clock somewhere, right?"

I smile. "It's only been one glass. I'm not going to overdo it." So me and wine are best friends. Sometimes, we get along too well, and I wake up in a wine-induced state.

"Just making sure. How was your day?"

I shrug and sip on my wine. "Busy. I have tomorrow off and we have to do some *major* cleaning!"

"Why?" he whines, taking my hand and walking me to the couch of our living room. Settling down, I place my wine glass on the table and bring my knees up to my chest. "Fine. But seriously, the house is clean, you OCD freak."

"I resent that comment. Sorry; I like to have a nice house, you know, for when we have company or stuff."

"Company? You never have them come over. It's always just Stephen."

I think about what he said. He's right. I don't have anyone come over. This house, my home, is my safe place. It's where I can come home after working and relax. It's where I talk to Brody and tell him about my day when I know he'll never answer back. If people come here, they may see his picture and ask about him. No one knows about my past in Montana except for Isaac. The wounds from my past can't come to surface. I buried them the day I buried Brody.

"I don't have him over. He invites himself and makes a mess!"

"He's coming over to watch baseball, so," he looks around the house, "spotless house."

"Fine," I groan. "But no mess, please?"

"Sure thing. Where you going?"

I get up from the couch, not able to sleep, even though I really want to. "Zumba class with Karly and Lexi. They made me sign up with them and I think it'll be a good idea. Right?"

"Thatta girl! Go shake it."

"Shake it? Please stop! You're my little brother and I don't want you thinking about me shaking anything."

"We're not biological bro and sis. No wonder Brody loved you so much." He winks, turning to the TV.

Walking into the studio, I notice several people in various groups, laughing and talking. I tug my workout bag closer to my body and try to find a place in the back so I'm not noticed. Settling on the floor, I spread out my legs in front of me and stretch. I've never done zumba before, but the girls at the hospital rave about it. I'm more of a runner than a "shake it" kind of girl. From the YouTube videos I watched, it seems fun. I just hope I'm coordinated enough to follow the moves.

"Hey!" Karly and Lexi find me and make their way over. "No, you're coming to the front!"

"No! Stop!" I beg. "I am the *least* coordinated person in this room. I cannot be in the front. I'll embarrass myself."

Before she can respond, the instructor walks in, turns on the stereo, and music fills the room. Looking in the mirror, watching my body move to the music, shaking my ass and raising my arms in the air, I forget about the pain. The dance is numbing the pain and it's really helping me let loose. I watch the instructor in the mirror and mimic her moves. It's easy to pick up on the dances and soon I'm not paying attention to her, but myself. The seductive and high-powered music pumps through the room and I let go.

I let go.

Carefully picking up my bags, I wince in pain and curse myself for doing this damn class. I didn't realize how much moving and shaking there is when it comes to zumba. Holy son of a...I need ice and lots of ice.

"I'm so sore!" I whine.

"You'll be fine." Lexi waves me off. "We're actually gonna grab something to eat. Wanna join us?"

I don't have anything else to do besides go home and rest. Plus, with Stephen going over to watch the game with Isaac, I feel like girl time is needed. We walk out of the studio to a little café. It's nice outside, so we decide to eat outside.

Vision of Hope

Ordering a Tuscan Panini and a bottle of water, I take out my phone and turn it on. A picture of Brody and me pops up.

"Ohhhhh, who is *that*? He is so hot!" Lexi takes my phone and shows it to Karly. "Wow, is he someone you like? Who is this?"

And there's the question I've been dreading. I freeze, not knowing what to say. I've only talked to Isaac about Brody. Keeping my eyes on Karly's hands while she's holding my phone, I think about what I can tell them. My mind doesn't register the question. I can't think or talk.

"Fallyn?" Karly calls for me. "You okay? You're so pale."

My order is called and I take my tray to the table outside. I rip the paper off my straw and stick it in my cup of lemonade. Covering the straw with my lips, I lean back and take a few healthy gulps. I need this moment to be alone before they come to the table and shoot their questions. I don't need anyone's pity or sympathy.

When I look up, they're looking at me, waiting for an answer I'm not sure how to give. "He's someone from my past. I love him, but we can't be together."

"I'm sorry." They reach over and take my hand. "We're here if you need to talk."

"Thanks." I smile. Hearing those words means so much and, hopefully, one day, I can talk about Brody without falling apart. But that'll happen when I'm ready.

Back at home, I'm holed up in my room. Sitting on top of my bed, I look around and pull out my laptop and search for different ways to decorate a bedroom. I want my room to be inviting and warm. I need to do something to get my mind off today.

The mention of Brody sends me into a corner. I'm trying my hardest not to break down. Clicking through some pictures, an idea comes to mind. Getting off my bed, I begin moving around the furniture in my room. Looking at my window, I decide to go outside and get fresh roses from my garden. Picking out a few red roses, I go back inside, grab some ribbon, and tie a knot around the flowers. Bringing a step stool to my room, I hang the bouquet freely by my window and admire the flowers. For some reason, roses bring me peace. Brody loved roses, red roses, so having these in my room feels as though I have a piece of him too.

My phone buzzes in my jean pocket. Picking up my phone, I see a text from Stephen.

Stephen: *I'm starving!*

Me: *Come over and I'll order pizza.*

Stephen: *I love you so much!!!!!*

I laugh, shake my head, and head out to the living room to call the pizza parlor. A few minutes later, Stephen comes in and sits on the couch with me. He rests his arm on my shoulders and gives me his *I'm up to no good* smile.

"What did you do?"

"I need a favor."

I groan. Ever since I've met Stephen, he's been a permanent pain in my side. We became close really fast and, even though he's hot and sexy, I look at him as my best friend. We spend a lot of time talking and hanging out. And I usually help him out of these *situations*, which drives me crazy.

"Do I need to pretend to be your girlfriend?" He nods. "When?"

"Tomorrow night," he firmly says. "She won't leave me the fuck alone."

I cock my head to the side. "Maybe if you didn't fuck women like they were toys, then we wouldn't be here."

The doorbell rings and Stephen jumps up. "Meet me tomorrow at my house. Five p.m. sharp. I'm hungry, so no more crazy girl talk!"

Chapter 5
Lisa

It's been so hard being on my own. Jensen couldn't make it this weekend, and it pisses me off that he's putting work before seeing me. He's the freaking medical director! He can make his own schedule and *make* other doctors work. I don't care if I'm being selfish. I'm here alone in Rochester while he's back in Wilmington with our family and friends.

Slamming my books closed, I get up and pace around the empty apartment. It's too quiet here and I'm going crazy. I wish I could have a roommate, but I need to stay focused and get through school. I keep telling myself that this is my decision and mine alone. I could have stayed in Wilmington and finished, but I want more. Plus Fisher is my dream school. Even though I have to start at the bottom, again, it's worth it.

I pick up my phone, hoping someone's around and wants to hang out, then I realize that they're in study groups now. I should be there too, but I wouldn't be able to focus. I need to be alone and read in peace; that's why I opted for no roommate.

Settling on the couch, I pick up the remote and scroll through to see what's on. I settle on *The Big Bang Theory* and try to take my mind off Jensen not being here.

A few hours later, the vibration of my phone wakes me up. It's almost six o'clock when I creep off the couch to get ready for my night class. Glancing at my phone, I see it's a text message from Jensen.

My Love: *Hey babe. I'm home now. Sorry that I didn't make it this weekend. I'll do everything I can to make it up to you. I promise. I love you, babe.*

I look at the text and decide not to text him back. Feeling hungry, I throw on my black PINK hoodie and head to campus for food before heading to my night class. A few of my friends are at the Fish Bowl when I walk in. We talk for a few moments before I grab my order of chicken fingers and fries and head outside to class. There are only about seven minutes before I have to get to class and if I don't make it on time, my professor will make the biggest scene. He hates it when we're late.

Before walking into class, I hear my name being called. Turning around, I nearly drop everything in my hands.

"Ian!?"

I haven't seen him since we broke up a few years ago. Shit, this is kind of weird.

"Hey!" He rushes over to me and gives me a hug. "Damn, it's been so long. What are you doing here?"

"I transferred here from UNCW. My grades got better and Fisher accepted me into their nursing program. I've been here for a while, actually." Looking at Ian, something in me wakes up. He looks older, hotter... Oh fuck, what am I doing? *Jensen! You're with Jensen! Stop looking into his gorgeous gray eyes or at his sexy sideways smile. Stop, Lisa! You have an amazing boyfriend!*

"That's awesome. Hey, I gotta run, but lunch or something soon." He hugs me again, kissing my cheek. "I'll talk to you later." He winks before running off.

Oh, this is not good. Not good at all.

Class goes by so slowly. I'm finding it hard to stay awake, but I also have other things on my mind, like seeing Ian. I can't stop thinking about him. We dated throughout high school, but broke up because, well, I don't really remember why we broke up. I think it was mutual and then we went our separate ways.

It's weird how we're both in the same place. I'm a firm believer in everything happens for a reason. So what's the reason for running into Ian? I have a few friends here, so I'm not lacking in that department. I don't have feelings for him anymore. Actually, I haven't thought about him since we broke up. These thoughts plague my head and it's driving me crazy.

When class is over, I head home and text Jensen. I need to get my mind off Ian.

Me: *Hi! Whatcha doing?*

My Love: *Reviewing some paperwork.*

Me: *Oh man, that sucks.*

My Love: *How was your day?*

I contemplate if I should tell him about Ian. But there's really no reason.

Me: *It was good. My three-hour class drained me.*

My Love: *I'm sorry about that. What else do you have planned for tonight?*

Me: *Studying my life away! Wish you were here....*

My Love: *I know, baby. I wish I could be there with you too. I'm sorry for not making it, but know that I'm thinking of you.*

Me: *I just miss you! I can't wait to see you soon!*

Jensen's coming up in a few days and, honestly, this is the perfect time. I think seeing him will push Ian out of my head.

I go through the next few days in a funk. I wake up, get ready, go to class, and come back home to study. Burying myself in homework and watching reruns isn't what I want to do, but call me crazy, it's bringing me comfort. When I'm keeping my mind busy and focusing, I'm not missing Jensen as much.

After finishing my paper, I get up from the chair and decide to go for a run. Throwing on yoga capris and a hoodie, I grab my ear buds and phone. Walking outside, I do a quick stretch and run.

Turning the corner, I see Ian and some of his friends walking towards me. Quickly, I move my eyes somewhere else, so I pretend as if I didn't see him.

"Lisa!" he shouts. I ignore him and continue running. He catches up to me and starts running alongside me. Damn it, Ian. Pulling out my ear buds, I turn my head to him and he smiles. "Mind stopping?"

"Okay." I stop running and turn off my music. "What's up?"

"Well, I tried texting you after we saw each other, but I guess you changed your number?"

"You still have my number from high school?"

"Yeah," he nervously answers. "I do. But like I said, you changed it."

"I did," I let him know. "What did you need?"

"Nothing major. Wanted to see if you wanted to get dinner or something. You know, catch up. We're going to the same school now and we might as well hang out."

He's right. We both go to the same school and it's not like anything's going to happen. We've both changed since high school and I'm happy with Jensen.

"You know what? That sounds really good. I haven't had dinner yet. Wanna grab something?"

"Yeah, for sure."

I smile. "Okay. Lemme go back home and get ready." I rattle off my address to him and give him my new number. "Give me an hour and come over."

"Sounds good. I'll see you soon."

"Okay." I watch him walk back to his friends and I put back in my ear buds and turn around to run back to my apartment.

* * * * *

Spending yesterday with Ian didn't feel weird. We talked and laughed. It felt normal to be near him again. I didn't get a chance to find out a lot about him because he wanted to know what I had been up to since high school. I filled him in and he listened. We were at Next Door Bar and Grill until one a.m. and he took me home and walked me to the front door of my apartment. It was weird when he said goodnight. He watched me walk inside and made me text him when I was inside my apartment.

After spending time with him, he's all I can think about. He texted me this morning around eight, but I haven't responded. I've been inside studying and finishing my paper. Almost five hours later, my brain is dead and I need a pick-me-up.

After I put on my shoes, I grab my keys and head out the door. I haven't been exploring Rochester, so I take the time to walk around campus and hopefully meet some people.

Heading to the Fish Bowl for no reason, I walk in and see Ian. Of course I would see him. Our eyes immediately meet and it's too late to leave. He waves me over and I smile and take a seat next to him.

"Hey, guys, this is an old friend from home. Lisa Presley." I wave and smile at the two other couples at the table. The girls are both blonde and look nice. The guys have athletic builds and it makes me wonder if Ian still plays soccer and if these are his friends from the team.

"So as I was saying," one of the guys says, "tomorrow's game is gonna be crazy."

"Playing Elmira College is gonna be tough," Ian adds. "But we'll get 'em."

"Are you coming tomorrow, Lisa?" one of the blondes ask. "We have room in the car if you wanna ride with us."

I look at her, then at Ian. He smiles and nods his head like he wants me to go. "Sure. Thanks for letting me tag along."

"I'm rude." Ian laughs. "Lisa, that's Brenda and Emmy and the guys, Chris and Eric. I play soccer with these two and they're dating these beauties."

"It's nice to meet you all."

During the next few hours, we have dinner and talk more. I like Brenda and Emmy. They have an apartment on Park Avenue and this is their last semester before student teaching. Part of me is envious. I'm supposed to be a senior too. Hopefully, I can convince my professors to give me letters of recommendations and I can be a second semester junior; even that'll make me happy.

I look at the time and see it's almost ten p.m. "I gotta get going, Ian. I have an early class tomorrow." I grab my purse and jacket. "It was nice meeting everyone again. I'll see you tomorrow." They wave and say bye.

Ian follows me, and when I turn around, he's inches from my face. "What are you doing?"

"Walking you to your car," he states. "It's late and I don't want you walking alone."

"Oh." I blush. He places his hand on my back and leads me down the slight hill to my car. "Thanks again, Ian. I'll see you tomorrow."

"Sounds good. Have a good night and sweet dreams." I raise my hand and wave, getting in my car and starting it. When I look up, Ian's still standing in the same spot. We hold our stare for a few moments before I put the car in reverse and leave.

Vision of Hope

Ian is on my mind during my drive back to my apartment and when I walk inside. My phone rings, alerting me of a text. When I pull it out, there's a text from Ian.

Ian: *Good seeing you again, Lisa =)*

Chapter 6
Jensen

It's been a long day and I'm ready to kick back and relax. Parking my car, I head inside to The Harp. I'm seated in a booth and look through the menu, waiting for Stephen to get here.

"What can I get ya?"

I look at the server and smile. "I need a few minutes. Meeting someone here."

"Gotcha." She winks, turning around to go to her next table.

Putting my attention back to the menu, I make my decision for dinner and pull out my phone.

Me: *Where the hell are you?*

Stephen: *Walking in, sweetie pie. You miss me ;)*

Stephen slides into the booth with Fallyn. I kink my brow and look at Stephen.

"Hey, Jensen," she says.

"Hey. What's up?"

I don't mind having Fallyn here. She's nice and comes around to hang with us every now and then. Besides knowing that she's one of my nurses at the hospital and best friends with Karly and Lexi, and she's Stephen's neighbor, I don't know too much more about her.

We've been in a few meetings together at the hospital. Other than that, we haven't talked too much since she's been in Wilmington. When Lexi brought her to one of our get-togethers, she kept to herself most of the night. I wasn't an asshole by any means, but I didn't take the time to get to know her.

"Nothing. Stephen dragged me out. Apparently, I'm not getting out enough."

"You aren't," Stephen answers, putting down his menu. "All you do is work and go home. You hardly hang out with us and it's a little upsetting. We see Isaac more than you."

"I have to agree with my man over here. I barely know you, besides knowing a few things like you're a nurse, your best friends with the girls, and you unfortunately live next door to idiot over there."

"Do you wanna break up with me or something?" Stephen says, holding his chest. "I'm hurt with all of this verbal abuse."

"Shut up, asshole." We laugh. "But on a serious note, why don't you come out?"

"I do," she stammers. "I'm busy with work. I've been pulling sixteen-hour shifts and I have a house to take care of. I don't know what else to tell you."

"But we don't need you to do that." There's slight irritation in my tone. I make sure that each department is adequately staffed so none of my employees are overworked. "What I mean is there's enough staff on your floor. You don't need to pull doubles and overwork yourself. It's important that you get enough rest so when you come back for your next shift you aren't overtired."

"Well, I've been taking people's shifts when they can't make it. It's fine, Jensen. I like working. And I know what I'm doing." She glares at me with a pointed look. "Trust me. I know."

"Fine, but please don't overwork yourself." I'm trying to think of something to ease the tension between us. "If you ever get too tired please let me know. I want to help you and don't want you to feel alone."

"Yes, sir," she smirks at me and I can't help but laugh.

The conversation goes well and soon we put in our order. I keep looking at Fallyn, trying to figure out her story. Her stubborn glare catches my attention. Her body is tense, making me curious.

Stephen: *Why are you staring?*
Me: *I'm not.*
Stephen: *Dude, I'm right here. What's up?*
Me: *Why does she seem uncomfortable?*
Stephen: *I've been trying to figure her out since she's been here. She's too closed up. Isaac doesn't say much either.*

Stephen's phone rings and interrupts our conversation. "Hey, sorry. I gotta take this call." Fallyn moves out of the booth and lets Stephen walk out. When she slides back in, I tilt my head to the side and try to read her a little more now that Stephen isn't around.

"I can feel you staring at me, you know."

"I'm sorry," I falter. "I don't mean to make you uncomfortable. Just trying to figure you out. You've been here for a while, but hardly come out and hang. I know that you're working a lot, but you can't use that as an excuse, so what's going on?"

"Really, nothing. I work a lot, like you said, and I'm tired. Being a nurse is hard. You should know what it's like to be working countless hours with little sleep. It gets to you."

"I do know what it's like, but I also know when someone is holding back a story." I'm not sure what possessed me to say that to her. Now I am definitely staring at her. She's holding back something and curiosity is getting to me.

There's a pause between us while we're waiting for Stephen, giving me plenty of time to study her before my girlfriend's brother comes back.

"So what else do you like to do besides work?'

Vision of Hope

"I signed up for Zumba classes with Karly and Lexi. In the mornings, or whenever I have time, I run about five to seven miles a day."

"I run a lot too. Where do you run?"

"Just down a few trails by my house, but running on the beach is my favorite. Living in Montana, I never saw the beach, and we didn't go on vacations, so living here is a plus."

"Yeah, I know what you mean. Since I've lived here, it's been incredible."

"The people are so nice and I really like Karly, Lexi, and you guys, of course. It's so different from Montana. I can't explain it, but it's a nice feeling. You know how you just feel like this is the place you need to be? Well, I feel that way. And the little shops around town and the little odds and ends around here are fun to explore." Her face turns pink and she blinks her eyes a few times. Her hair flutters to her face and she uses her index finger to curl the strand behind her ear. "I just rambled, didn't I?"

Her gaze meets mine again. "Yeah, you did, but I didn't mind. It was nice hearing you talk. You're always quiet. You should change that. You're fun to be around."

"This is the first time we're really hanging out."

"And I'd like to hang out with you more often. We work together, so we should get together for lunch."

"Okay. Sounds fun."

Stephen comes back when Fallyn agrees to hang out with me. The three of us eat our dinner and she stays quiet for the rest of the night.

Heading back home after dinner, I feel restless and need to tire myself out. Changing out of my clothes, I put on sweats and a white tee and head out to my car. The drive to the gym is quick. When I walk inside, I put my things in the locker in the men's room and walk back out. Hopping on the treadmill, I put on my ear buds and set the speed to start running.

Finishing six miles without a problem, I wipe down the treadmill and head to the weights. It's been a week since I've been in the gym. Grabbing some weights, I take a seat on the bench and work on my arms. Looking at myself in the mirror for form and focusing on my breathing, I finish the last set and realize Fallyn's over in the corner, doing squats. My eyes shouldn't be on her ass and I shouldn't care that we're both working out together. So why am I getting up and walking over to her?

"Hey."

She looks up. "Hey, Jensen. Late-night workout?"

"Yeah, couldn't sleep and wanted to tire myself out. I don't think I've seen you here before."

"I work out at weird times," she answers me and turns back to finish her squats. Her form is near perfect and I go into trainer mode.

"You have really good form. How many sets are you doing?"

"Five," she says. "Are you a trainer or something?"

"Back in college, I use to work at the gym in college. I like training and working out."

"Oh, wow, I didn't know that about you. You're in really good shape. I thought it was genetics." She laughs, and I like the sound of her laughing.

"We should come and workout together sometimes."

"I'd like that. I gotta get going, though. I'll talk to you later."

I nod. "See you tomorrow morning."

Fallyn walks away and I'm looking forward to our workout session. Usually, I go with Stephen, but he's been busy with work and Lexi and Karly stick to cardio and Zumba. It'll be nice to lift with someone else.

The next morning I get up early and head out for a run. For the first time in a while I slept pretty well and didn't have the

Vision of Hope

weight of the world on my shoulders. With the music blasting in my ears I focus on running, feeling the blood circulating through my body, and the burning in my legs. Turning a corner, I see Fallyn coming my way. She looks focused and doesn't see me. She's getting closer and I'm not sure why, but I'm staring at her body. Damn.

"Jensen!" I look up and hope she didn't notice me staring. "Hey."

We both stop and take off our ear buds. "Good morning."

"You're up really early."

"Yeah," I answer, turning off the music on my iPhone. "I slept pretty well last night and woke up energized. Not sure why," we both laugh, "Are you almost done?"

"Not really. I'm in the same boat. Last night I slept so well and now I have all this energy. Mind if I join you?"

"Yeah," I smile, "Sure come on."

We carry a light conversation about work and our day. In the corner of my eye I notice Fallyn and how focused she is while running. This girl has an amazing body and she works out like crazy. Her curves are sexy and that ass.

Shit! What the fuck. Stop staring at her. You have a fucking girlfriend.

After our run, I tell Fallyn I'll see her at work and head home. She doesn't live too far from me, but I have to hurry or else I'll miss my eight a.m., meeting. Rushing my shower, I quickly get ready, grab my things and am out the door.

I make it to the conference room with a few minutes to spare and sit down, taking out notes and my phone.

"Morning." I look up and see a smiling Fallyn. She's holding two cups of coffee. "I figured you wouldn't have time to get a cup so I brought you one." She hands me the cup along with a small paper bag with cream and sugar.

"I like my coffee black," I tell her, "But thank you for doing this. You're a lifesaver."

"I try."

The meeting goes by quickly. I check my schedule on my iPhone and prepare for my next one.

"If you're not busy for lunch do you want to get sushi?"

Fallyn and I walk out of the conference room together and walk to the elevator. "Sure. I should be ready at around 12:30? Does that sound good?"

"Sure does." The elevator dings and we both get on. "Floor?"

"Five."

"Do you have a meeting now?" I nod, "Me too. Looks like our day is going to be fun."

I can't help to laugh. She hums a song, swaying from side to side. She's beautiful and so carefree. I know I'm watching from the corner of my eye.

"You'll have to tell me your story."

"I kinda did," she laughs, playing with the files in her hands. "There's not much to tell. I mean I think it's lame to sit there and tell someone about themselves. Get to know me by hanging out with me."

"Ahhh if this is your way to tell me you want to hang out more without actually telling me then game on, Phillips."

We both laugh, shaking our heads, and I realize how easy it is to be around her. I'm not sure if this is a good thing or bad thing, especially when I haven't thought about Lisa since this morning with Fallyn.

Chapter 7
Fallyn

"So are you gonna get that dress?" Lexi asks, pushing through the dresses on the rack. "I mean, it looks amazing on you. You have an ass and boobs that you need to flaunt."

I thumb through the dresses on the rack and keep looking at the one I have over my arm. It's nice, but I'm not sure how it's going to look on me. I haven't gotten dressed up like this in so long. Part of me is nervous. "Why are we going out tonight?"

"Because, for the hundredth time, we all have babysitters tonight—well, I mean Nicholas' parents are watching all the kids—and it's time we go out and have fun. We're more than just mommies and daddies, and you need to get out too! You have off tomorrow!"

I'm not in the mood to hang out at the bar tonight. Sitting down on the couch with my Kindle and some wine and chocolates sounds so much better than getting ready and going out. Many things go through my head like *Am I going to dance? What do I do if someone comes up and dances with me? Am I going to have fun? Would Brody want me to go out and have fun?*

"Stephen's driving y'all. Right?" I nod. "Oh, I think Jensen's coming tonight too. He was supposed to go up to see Lisa this weekend, but they're fighting yet again." She rolls her eyes. At that moment, I close my eyes and think about the get-togethers we've been having. It's been innocent and fun. We meet for lunch at different places like for sushi, subs, or grabbing a hot dog and walking around the town. He talks about Lisa sometimes and I listen. There's usually sadness when he talks about her, but he didn't mention their fight.

He's been helping me work out and it's been really helpful. I already see a difference with my energy level and I look forward to going to the gym.

"Earth to Fallyn! What's with your dreamy look? Oh my God! Did you meet someone?"

Instantly, I feel my body tense. "What? Who? NO!"

"Then what's going on?"

I roll my eyes. "Nothing. I was just thinking about tonight. Why are you asking?"

"Hmmm, defensive." She shakes her head. "Well, I think you met someone, and whoever this person is, don't let them go. You're smiling a lot more."

I close my eyes and wish for her to stop talking about how I'm feeling or how I look. I don't see a difference. I'm the same old Fallyn Nicole Phillips. Nothing new, nothing old. Just me. But there's a small part of me that is wondering what she's talking about. I didn't meet anyone new. Sure, Jensen and I are friends, but that's how I see him. This dreamy look she's talking about is stupid. I need to stop letting her words get to me. I'm over thinking.

"Are you gonna get the dress?"

"I guess I don't see anything else I like."

"Perfect! Come on!"

We pay for our clothes and head out of the store. Lexi looks at her watch and instantly freezes. "Shit! I gotta go and get ready!"

"It's only seven, though."

"Exactly! Listen, me and Larry haven't had a night alone in a while, so I need to make sure I'm all fresh and clean because I need sex and hot sucking, licking, and fucking tonight."

"I really didn't need to hear all of that." I grimace.

"Just because my vagina is in commission and yours isn't because you're so closed off on men for whatever reason doesn't mean I can't tell my best friend about my night." She winks, blows me a kiss, and walks away.

If only she knew why I'm so closed off on men. I'm dreading tonight and hope that it's at least fun. But who am I kidding? I know tonight's going to be fun and that scares me. Living again, to me, means I'm okay without Brody and I'm not. I wish he were here with me. He'd like my new friends.

Getting in my car, I drive home. My mind keeps going to tonight. "So I'm going out tonight." I say to no one. "I have no idea what to expect, but it should be fun, right?"

I know no one's going to answer. It's nice to talk as if he's next to me. "Well, wish me luck tonight and let's pray I don't make a fool of myself."

When I get home, I immediately go to the bathroom and hop into the shower. I take my time shampooing and conditioning and shaving. Even though I have no interest with hooking up with anyone, at least I can look and feel pretty.

Drying off, I plug in my hairdryer and style my hair. When I get out my makeup, I try something different. Pulling up YouTube and searching for *smoky eye tutorial,* I watch the short clip and repeat it so I can follow along.

Over an hour getting ready and pretty; I snap a few selfies and send them to the girls.

Karly: *Holy shit! You look so hot!*

Lexi: *I think I just came! Wow, Fallyn!*

I look in the mirror and groan. Closing my eyes, I tip my head back. "Brody, I hope you're having fun watching me get ready. You know I never take this long. But do I look pretty?" There is a knock on the door and it opens. Isaac stands in front of me and smiles from ear to ear.

"Not gonna lie, but you look damn hot tonight. This is the Fallyn I miss." He touches my arm, making his way down to my hand. "I know it won't be easy tonight, but we're gonna have fun."

I smile and nod my head. Fun. Right. We're going to have fun. When Stephen gets to the house, he opens a bottle of Patron and pours us shots. I look at the shot of death and cringe. I haven't drunk in so long, let alone getting wasted off of hard liquor. Where's my wine?

"To a good night, friends," he smirks and winks at me. We take the shot at once and I swear I feel my insides burning. Stephen pours more, but I don't protest. I take each one just like the guys.

* * * * *

Pravda Nightclub is packed tonight. The music is blasting and the drinks are endless. The guys got a VIP booth with bottle service. I guess when they party, they really party. Pitbull and Ne Yo "Time of Our Lives" plays, bringing me, Lexi, and Karly to the dance floor. The three of us are wearing dresses; short, but classy. About midway through, Nicholas, Stephen, and Larry join us. I look to the booth and see Isaac and Jensen drinking and laughing. My eyes stay on Jensen's as I dance. I feel Stephen coming behind me, wrapping his arm around my waist, and we move together. He's a really good dancer. Good Lord!

"I like that dress on you," he whispers in my ear. "You sure you don't want some of this?"

I laugh, shaking my head, and continue dancing with him.

"Shots!" Lexi yells, passing us all glasses of clear liquid. We raise our shot glasses in the air and take it together. "Wooooo," she yells, grabbing my hand and bringing me in front of her as Karly dances behind her.

I'm letting go.

I'm having fun.

Vision of Hope

See, Brody? I can have fun and I'm living.

The night is turning out better than I thought. We're up in the VIP lounge, talking and having fun. Isaac's by my side and won't leave me alone.

"I'll be fine. Go have fun." He puts his arm around me. "Honestly, I am. I'm glad we decided to come out." He hands me another drink, and we clink glasses and drink.

Karly squeezes between us and looks at Isaac then me. "So you two are..." she pauses, "what?"

I shake my head and laugh. Seeing Karly drunk is too much. "She's my best friend," Isaac fills her in, "We grew up together in Montana and now here I am."

"Oh my gosh so you followed her. Oh my gosh do you like her?" She turns to me, "Do you like him?"

"No," we both answer in unison.

"Just friends, Karly," I tell her, "Plus I already told you about Isaac."

"Ohhhh," she tilts her head back, rubbing her chin. "Yep okay. Got it."

Isaac leans over and mouths to me *Is she okay?* I shrug and laugh. Tonight is definitely what I needed.

The music gets louder, which causes us to get up and dance. Joining Lexi and Karly by the railing, we dance to the music, and laugh with one another. The guys are behind us, enjoying the little show of us being silly and trying to be sexy. When I nearly fall on my ass – thank you, vodka – Jensen quickly hurries to me and helps me before I fall.

"Thanks." I smile, holding on to his arm. "I think I had too much to drink."

He laughs, agreeing with me. "Sit down and I'll get you water."

"Okay."

Jensen hands me a bottle of water and sits down next to me. I look at everyone else and see that they're doing shots and talking. Putting my feet on the couch, I stretch out my legs and think about falling asleep. This couch is so comfortable.

"No sleeping!" Jensen laughs. "Come on and dance with me." He takes my hand and leads the way. Everyone else follows and soon we're on the dance floor again. I ignore the pain shouting from my feet and let the music take control.

We dance together in a group, laughing and throwing our arms in the air. Jensen's close to me and I can feel the heat radiating from his body. He takes my hand and twirls me around, making me laugh from how silly we all look. Everyone around us is grinding and pretty much having sex on the dance floor while we're doing the most ridiculous dances.

"Are you having fun?" He shouts.

I nod, "So much fun! Glad I came out tonight!"

"Me too!"

The songs keep us moving through the night along with the alcohol. By the time the club closes we're all stumbling out of the club and decide that taking a cab back home is the best thing.

Karly, Nicholas, Lexi and Larry take one cab home while me, Jensen, Stephen and Isaac take another.

"Call me tomorrow!" Karly says, "I love you bitch! Glad you came out tonight."

I smile and wave, getting in the backseat of the cab. When Stephen rattles off our address I lean my head to the right and loop my arm through Isaac's arm.

"Thanks for making me go out tonight, Isaac. I had fun," I mutter.

"I'm glad. Shhh go to sleep."

That isn't Isaac.

Chapter 8
Jensen

Me: *Good morning, sleepy head. Are we meeting up for a run?*

Fallyn: *It's 8 am. I just got to bed at 5 am after throwing up everything plus some. Are you seriously asking me to go running with you?*

Me: *Yeah why not?*

Fallyn: *Because I'm fucking hungover!*

Me: *Get your ass up and open the door for me!*

Fallyn: *I'm going to kill you. You're going to die a slow and painful death.*

In a few moments, the door opens and I'm shocked to see her and the sleepy look on her face. Her hair is a mess and I'm pretty sure she's still wearing the makeup from last night.

"Well, don't you look beautiful, darling."

"Shut up," she answers, leaving me at the door. She walks to the kitchen and pulls out two bottles of water. "I'm gonna take a quick shower because I think I smell like vodka with a mix of juices."

"Okay, sounds good. See you in a few hours." I laugh and she turns to give me a dirty look. Pulling out two coffee mugs and popping a K cup in the Keurig, I make her a cup of coffee and also one for myself.

Feeling comfortable in her kitchen, I take out two containers of oatmeal and granola with a Greek yogurt. Putting everything out on the counter for her, I turn around and head into the living room. Sitting on the couch, I pull out my phone and notice a few text messages.

Stephen: *Dude, never again. I'm not fucking 18 anymore.*

Lisa: *I heard you went out to the club last night. Not sure how you can manage to do that and NOT come see me. Whatever. I'm done. This is so stupid. I hate you!*

This is exactly how I want to start my morning. Pressing Lisa's contact information and then pressing the phone icon, I bring my phone to my ear and wait for her to answer.

"Do you not know what 'I'm done' means?"

"Stop acting like a brat. We've been fighting all week. I tried asking you if it was okay to come see you this weekend. You never answered."

"Oh, so this is my fault now? Nice, Jensen. You should have known just to freaking come and see me. I miss you and I'm trying to be okay with us not spending time together, but when I fucking find out you went clubbing and didn't even tell me, it's like what the hell. Are you doing something you're not supposed to do?"

"And what would that be, Lisa?"

"I don't know. Why are you at the club?"

I let out a breath of frustration and curse myself for going. To a degree, she has a point. A very small degree. "I went out with everyone. It's been a long-ass week and the kids were with Nicholas' parents. Like I said, I didn't know that this weekend would be good for you, Lisa. What the hell do you want from me? I'm trying here."

"Why the hell do you think it's okay to go out like that? And I have to find out on Facebook! Oh, and the picture of you and Fallyn is cute."

Who the hell took pictures? I think about last night and remember Karly and how her phone was attached to her hand.

"She's a friend. Why are you upset?"

"She's a very *single* friend! You have the biggest freaking smile on your face and you're hugging her from behind! That's a boyfriend and girlfriend pose, Jensen."

"Do you hear yourself?" I get up from the couch and pace the room. "Really, do you hear yourself right now? It was a *picture* and we danced and I had fun. Sorry that I couldn't make it to see you, but do not sit there and accuse me of doing things when I haven't done anything!"

I'm in a losing battle with her. Nothing I say will make the situation better.

"I don't know what to say. I didn't do anything and I've apologized. You can either take it or stay pissed at me because, at this point, I have no idea what you want."

I hear her breathing on the other end. Neither of us says anything. I'm not sure what we can say.

"If you can make it for a night, that'll be good."

"I'll try and see if I can get a flight out."

"Just let me know."

"Okay."

"Okay."

The call ends and I'm about five seconds from throwing my phone against the wall when I feel hands on my shoulders. I let out a breath and turn around.

"Let's go for that run."

* * * * *

Getting off my plane and walking through the Rochester airport, I see Lisa by the doors, waiting for me. She's not smiling and her arms are crossed around her chest. She's wearing yoga pants and a hoodie and looks like shit, to be honest.

Walking over to her, I put down my bag and bring her in my arms. "Hey."

"Hi."

To say the feeling between us is off is an understatement. Something's off and I think we're both pulling away from each other. As much as I know I love her, the love I have for her might not be as strong as it used to be.

"Come on. Let's head back to your apartment." I pick up my bag, place my hand on the small part of her back, and we walk out.

The drive to her apartment is quiet as she drives her car off the highway and turns into her apartment complex. I'm not sure where to start or what to say. I love her, but again, how strong is my love for her?

Before she cuts the engine, she turns around in her seat and looks at me. "What's going on with us?"

"I don't know, babe. I've been asking myself the same thing. I don't know what you want anymore and everything I do is wrong in your eyes. You're constantly picking fights with me…"

"Because I need you here with me!"

"And I am trying my best!" I yell. Instantly getting out of her car, I push my hands in my hair and bend my head down. I don't yell at Lisa, ever. This isn't how I want to be or treat her.

"Jensen, come inside so we can talk."

"I need a minute."

"Jensen, what the fuck. Just come inside."

I turn around and look at her. "Lisa, gimme a minute. Go up and I'll be there in a few minutes."

"Fine. Whatever."

I watch her walk inside her complex and all I can think about is my irritation. I shouldn't feel this way about the woman I love. It has to be the distance that's hurting us. Taking a few deep breaths, I calm down and look back at the building. I love her and I want to spend my life with her. This

Vision of Hope

is an obstacle we have to overcome and we will. I'll try harder and she'll soon see that.

Pulling out my phone I text Fallyn. I have no idea what I'm doing or what I should do.

Fallyn: *Give her time, Jensen..The both of you need to relax and be calm..Don't talk out of anger and frustration*

Me: *But she's not fucking listening..I have no idea what I'm doing or why I'm doing this shit..She doesn't get it*

Fallyn: *Then make her understand*

I grumble under my breath and put my phone back in my jeans. Love isn't supposed to be this hard.

Walking towards her apartment I take the stairs two at a time and stand in front of the door. I contemplate what I should say and what I should do. Placing my hand on the doorknob I twist it, opening the door, and walking inside.

Lisa's sitting at the table with a cup in her hands. I sit down across from her and neither of us says anything. There's questions going through my head, but is it the right time to ask her.

"What are we doing?" She asks, beating me to asking my question first.

"Honestly I don't know. I know that I love you and I want to make this work. You need to understand I can't drop everything to come see you. I support your decision and want you to do well here. I have a life back home too, Lisa."

"I know," she mumbles, "I know. It's hard for me too. Sometimes I feel like you don't love me and if you do it's not as strong."

I don't respond. Part of me thinks she's right. Our love isn't as strong as before. "I'm willing to make this work between us. We've been through a lot, Lisa." I take her hand, rubbing it with my thumb. "Sometimes I feel like you're taking me for granted and you don't get where I'm coming from."

"I know. Because I don't. I want you here with me and I want you to understand how hard it is for me to be away."

She gets up from the table, wiping her eyes with her sleeves. I stay seated and hang my head. "I have no idea what you want. Please tell me."

"I shouldn't have to tell you!" She screams, "You should know!"

"Well I don't fucking know, Lisa!"

We're both standing in front of each other. Her tears fall from her eyes and my fists are clenched at my side. Coming here proves how pointless it is to be with her. Fuck what the hell am I going to do?

Chapter 9
Fallyn

I've been lying in bed for the past hour staring at my ceiling. It's nearly midnight and even though I have off tomorrow I still have a lot to do. Like cleaning and going for a run. My life is awesome.

Getting my phone from my nightstand I open Facebook and scroll through my newsfeed, liking some statuses and sharing a funny picture, tagging Karly and Lexi. Still scrolling I still Jensen's status and he's tagged himself at the airport. I wonder why he's coming back so soon.

Me: *How was the trip to see Lisa?*

Jensen: *Waste of time.*

Me: *Why?*

Jensen: *We fought the whole time and she cried, saying that I don't love her and shit. I was ready to walk away. I don't know what else she wants. I tried holding her, but she pushed me away.*

Me: *Long distance is hard, and she needs to know that you care. Where are you now?*

Jensen: *About to board. I'll ttyl.*

Me: *Safe travels! =)*

He didn't respond and I didn't expect him to. Hopefully they'll work it out. Lately he's been on edge, and I've been trying to get him to talk so he's not bottling in all of his emotions. Poor guy. It can't be easy having a long distance relationship.

I can't stand being in my room anymore. Pulling the covers off I put on my robe and see if Isaac's in his room. Peeking my head in I notice his bed is still made.

Me: *Hey are you out?*

Isaac: *Grabbing beer and food with a few people. You ok?*

Me: *Yeah, yeah..Fine..Just can't sleep..Wanted to see where you were =)*

Isaac: *Lol I'm fine..I'll see you tomorrow*

Me: *K*

Walking around the quiet house, I'm not sure what to do. Flopping on the couch, I turn on the TV and flip the channels. "Oh *Law and Order*." Grabbing a pillow, I get comfortable on the couch and watch the episode, which I've seen a few times already. Letting out a sigh I turn off the TV and head back to my room. I can't focus or enjoy the time to myself. There are too many things going through my head. None of it makes sense.

I open my closet and pull out the box from the top shelf. Settling on my bed, I pull off the cover and pull out the letters. Letters between me and Brody. I pull out the last one he wrote me.

Hi, Fallyn,

You're sleeping next to me and you're snoring. I want to put a pillow over your head, but then that'll cover your beautiful face.

I've been watching you for a few hours. I can't sleep. I can't stop thinking about forever with you. We're going to have the most amazing wedding and I can't wait to dance to "Mine Would Be You." You'll always be my first choice, everything you are, everything you'll be. It doesn't matter because I'll love everything about you forever.

Vision of Hope

I can't wait to see you walk to me in your wedding dress. I can't wait for it all. Just so you know, the first time we make love as husband and wife, I'm getting you pregnant =)

Okay, baby, I'm going to watch you sleep some more.

I love you. Forever and always.

Your future baby daddy,

Brody

I laugh as I read his letter. Bringing the letter to my chest, I hold it tightly and let the tears stream down my face. "I miss you so much, Brody."

After Brody died, I felt lost and a piece of who I used to be was gone. My dreams and ambitions turned into blank spaces. However, leaving Montana, and putting the past behind me helped a bit. I threw myself into work and forced myself to be the woman I used to be. Slowly it was coming back to me and I was thankful. I hated the feeling of being alone and not enjoying the life I have.

Each day that passes gets a little easier, until I'm brought back to the past and remember him and our love. I think about going back to visit and soon I will. I can't now and the guilt worsens. It'll take time, I get that, it's the fear of losing myself that's stopping me.

Not being able to take more crying, I close the box and strip out of my clothes, walking into the bathroom and running a bath. I pour lavender bath salts and slowly step in. Letting the water fill my tub, I lean back and close my eyes. In my mind, I'm happy and I have a smile on my face. I'm in an open field and the sun is shining down on my face. I'm twirling around and my lips are moving, but I don't hear what I'm saying. Arms wrap about me and spin me around. I'm laughing so hard that I'm crying. I can't see who is holding me. I feel safe, though.

I wake up to a text the next morning and curse under my breath.

Stephen: *Wanna get breakfast?*

I groan when I realize it's seven in the morning. I'm going to kill Stephen for texting me so early on my day off!

Me: *You do realize what time it is right! Ugh!*

Stephen: *You love me...Get up so we can go..Heading over to your place now so get ready.*

Me: *K.*

Getting out of my bed, I walk into my bathroom and get ready for the day. After I'm done getting ready, I walk out to the living room and find Stephen sitting on the loveseat with sweats on. He looks up at me and there's sadness in his usually happy eyes.

"What's wrong?" I sit on the coffee table, facing him, placing my hands on his knees. "What's wrong?"

"Have you ever felt like the world was crashing in front of you and you have nowhere to go?"

I know that feeling all too well.

"Yeah, I do. You're scaring me. What's going on?"

"A woman I slept with a few times called me last night. She said she needed to talk to me and I thought she wanted to have sex, so I told her to come over." He pauses and leans back against the chair. "What I didn't expect was her to tell me she was pregnant."

"Was?"

He nods. "Yeah. She lost the baby and she said she needed me. I was confused and pissed because we slept together a few times and didn't have any real connections. I asked her why she was telling me and what difference it would make. She looked me dead in my eyes and said I was a heartless asshole and she was glad she lost the baby so she wouldn't be reminded of me. She slapped me and stormed out."

Vision of Hope

I know Stephen isn't ready for kids and I always tell him to be careful. Hearing how callous he was towards her upsets me. I know Stephen and I know he would have loved his child regardless of his initial reaction.

"Now I feel like a fucking asshole. I think about all the women I've fucked over the years. I think about all the *what if's* and wonder if I have kids out there."

"I don't wanna be a bitch, but I've told you before to be careful and you need to treat women better."

"I know. I guess what she said is fucking with my head. She was carrying my child and lost him or her and I'm sitting here with no feelings. Am I heartless?"

"No." I shake my head. "You're human and this is normal," I start to say, "You're going to have to change or else you'll never be happy."

"You're right," he mutters.

"Come on." I pull him up from the loveseat. "Breakfast is on me today."

When we're done with breakfast I advise Stephen to talk to her. He has a sad look in his eyes, but nods his head and leaves. Opening the front door, I go inside and find Isaac in the living room. He's holding his phone and his head is hanging low.

"What's wrong?" I hurry over and kneel down, taking his hands in mine.

"Just a shitty day," he sighs, squeezing my hands. I feel tears fall on my hands and instantly I cry too.

Part of me will always be guilty for having Isaac with me. He's been what I need since losing Brody. I feel like having Isaac here means I have a piece of Brody. For both of us leaving wasn't easy.

I've known Isaac since knowing Brody. He's the little brother I've always wanted and I don't know what I'd do without him.

"Talk to me, please."

"I miss him, sis. I talked to my dad today and I don't know. They seem okay and then we got talking to Brody and he asked about his car and what he should do with it." He cries, pulling me from the floor and onto the couch. I hold Isaac in my arms, rocking him back and forth. "I told him I had no idea. Brody loved his car. Do you remember how many hours we spent working on it?" I nod, remembering how happy Brody was to find the Mustang and vowed to bring it back to life and he did. "He only drove it a few times."

"I know."

"I miss him and I think I have to go back home to see how my parents are doing ya know?"

"I miss him too, honey. Every day. And I think that'll be a good thing. Don't feel like you have to be here for me. I'll be okay."

"I promised Brody, the day of his funeral, that I would watch over you."

"Isaac," I sigh, holding him tighter. "We'll be okay."

We stay like this for a while and soon we're both cried out. I need to get out of the house and go for a run. Isaac decides to order take out for the both of us.

My feet pounding against the pavement, the air hitting my face, the music in my ears, numbs the burning in my chest. But the fresh wounds of losing Brody are slowly opening. Images from that night play back in my head. I can hear his voice in my head and feel the weight of his body in my arms.

"I love you, Fallyn. I'm sorry I can't give you a forever."

"Brody, please fight. Please! I can't do this without you. You're my life!"

My body fails, and I fall to the ground. Pain surges through my arm and wrist. I roll on my back, take off my ear buds, holding my wrist to my chest.

"Fuck," I mutter, "Ugh." Slowly getting up I turn around and head home.

"Fallyn!" I turn and see Jensen getting out of his car and running towards me. "Are you okay?"

"Jensen? Why aren't you at work?"

"Took today off. But are you okay?" I nod, still holding my wrist to my chest. "Come on let me drive you home." I nod again, not able to talk.

Jensen helps me into his car. I lean my head back on the headrest, looking out the window. I hate how I've been doing somewhat fine and then this happens. I know that my emotions are going to be all over the place, but part of me wants to be okay. I've accepted he's not coming back and I know that. It still doesn't make it easier though.

"Where's your head at?"

I turn to face him and try to find my voice. "Just thinking about things. Thanks for taking me home. It's not necessary."

"Not a big deal," he pats my thigh and instantly my body relaxes. *Weird.*

When he pulls up and parks his car in my driveway, we sit in silence for a few seconds before I start talking. "Thank you again for helping me out. I appreciate it. I'd invite you in, but Isaac and I are having a little catch up session."

"Oh. So are you two..."

I burst out laughing. I have no idea why people think we're together. "No! No! He's my best friend. We grew up together. Why does *everyone* think we're together!"

"Because he lives with you and you two are together a lot. I don't know. I assumed, sorry."

"Don't be. Just don't go assuming things and come to me if you have questions." It's comfortable talking to Jensen and I'm actually a little bummed to not have him come in. "I'll see you later. Thanks again."

"No problem. Have fun.

Chapter 10
Jensen

Parking my car behind Stephen's, I open my car door and head inside to join everyone in Nicholas and Karly's house for our weekly get together. I open the door and hear laughter. A beautiful little girl runs down the hall and into my arms.

"Hi, beautiful." I hold her a little tighter, holding her head against my cheek.

"Hi, Uncle Jensen."

"How are you?"

"Good." She giggles. I lift her in the air and carry her into the kitchen.

"Jensen!" Karly and Lexi jump up and down and come over to me. "Finally, you made it."

"Yep, I'm here." I put Emma down and watch her run to Nicholas. I'll admit it hurts. I remind myself why I'm doing this and why this is the best thing for her.

Looking around the kitchen, I see Fallyn and Stephen on the couch, talking. I wonder what they're talking about. Taking a beer from the fridge, I join Nicholas and Larry, but I don't take my eye off of them. She seems to be more relaxed with Stephen than with me. It shouldn't bother me that he can make her laugh and smile. When we hang out, she seems more reserved.

"There you are, man! Didn't think you'd make it tonight."

"I'm here." I nod at Fallyn and see her smile.

"Where's my nod?" I blow Stephen a kiss and he catches it in the air. "See? He loves me." We laugh and Fallyn snorts while laughing and falls back into her chair.

"Did you just snort?"

She shakes her head and snorts again. "I'm," she can't stop laughing, "sorry. I'm sorry, but you two are really funny."

Stephen and I shrug. "As you girls say, 'it's a best friend thing.'"

The rest of the night, we hang out on the deck and Nicholas starts a bonfire. The girls— Karly, Lexi and Fallyn— are on the grass making s'mores while me and the guys are drinking beer and talking baseball.

From the corner of my eye, I see Fallyn is laughing and relaxed. The glimmer in her eyes and crinkle to her nose when she smiles are intoxicating. We've been talking and hanging out a little more. She listens when I talk about Lisa and gives me really helpful advice. As for Lisa and me, well, I still have no idea what's going on between us. It's clear that something's wrong and I'm trying hard to figure it out. She won't let me in and she refuses to talk about how she feels. If only I can be there for her the way she wants me to. There's not enough time in the day to finish my work and fly to Rochester.

"Hey man. How's everything going?" Isaac comes next to me.

"Good," I clink my beer bottle with his, "What's going on with you?"

"Same old. Thinking about heading back to Montana for a few days. Not sure yet."

"Ahhh sounds like fun. Everything okay?"

"Yeah, man. Nothing major. My parents are still there and I miss him," he laughs, drinking his beer. "Are things okay with you? Seem kind of stressed."

"Yeah," I rub the back of my neck, "Girlfriend issues."

"Say no more. Thank God I'm single." We laugh, and finish off our beers. "Need another?"

"Sure, thanks."

Isaac and I head to the cooler to grab more beers before joining the rest of the guys and head to the fire. Tonight's a much-needed night to relax and not worry about the stress of Lisa. I pull out my phone and check for any new messages. There's still nothing from Lisa. What the hell do I have to do to get her to stop being mad?

I walk inside and call her, but no answer. After leaving her a message telling her how much I miss and love her, I disconnect the call and turn back to leave. I'm about to walk outside when I see Fallyn coming inside.

"Hey," I say, raising my hand.

"Hey! What's up?"

"Nothing." I wave my phone in the air, and then put it back in my pocket. "I tried calling Lisa, but no answer."

She sits on the barstool and looks at me. "I'm sorry. I thought you two were doing okay or working on it. What's going on now?"

I groan. "I don't know. She's pissed because it's not easy for me to leave. She's not understanding that my work is important and I can't just pick up and leave. I'd love to be there with her and spend time with her. I don't know what to do so that she understands. It's the same thing over and over again. I don't know what else to do."

Fallyn stares at me and I can see the questions going through her head. "Just keep telling her how much you love her and that she means a lot to you. Girls need to know that they're wanted and cherished. If she doesn't understand where you're coming from, then explain it to her."

I take in what she's saying and realize that maybe I'm not telling Lisa what she means to me enough.

"Thanks, Fallyn. So, ah, I didn't want to ask you this, but are you and Stephen a thing now?"

Her eyes go wide and she laughs. "Oh God, no. He's a really good friend, but I'm not looking for anything."

"Why?"

Her body freezes and there's a distant look in her eyes. I'm not sure what emotion I stroked, but it seems pretty ugly. "I'm devoted to my work and, right now, I'm not ready to date anyone."

"Well, if you ever need to talk or need someone to vent to, I'm here for you."

"Thanks, Jensen. That means a lot."

I round the counter and give her a hug. I'm not sure what's making me do this, but hugs are awesome and usually make people feel better.

* * * * *

Me: *I'm home, babe. I hope you're doing okay. I miss you like crazy and love you so much. Please know that.*

Lisa: *I know and I'm sorry for ignoring you. It's hard when you aren't here. I need you so badly.*

Me: *I know. I need you too. But you can't push me away when you're upset. We need to talk out our issues before it blows up. Can you promise me you'll talk to me when things start getting hard?*

Lisa: *I promise to try. But it's hard and you need to realize that.*

Me: *I do realize that. And you need to realize that sometimes I can't just pick up and leave. Yes, I have a high position at the hospital, but things sometimes happen and I'm needed. When I'm able to go, it'll be worth it ;)*

Lisa: *I know and I do understand. Go to sleep, k? I love you.*

Me: *I love you too.*

I drop my phone in my lap, leaning against the headboard, and I close my eyes. Feeling frustrated, I think about buying a plane ticket now and seeing her, even if it's just for a few hours. She says she's going to try and I want to believe her. But I know Lisa. When things get hard, she pulls away. It's easier to pull her back when she's here and it usually doesn't take too much to remind her of our love and how perfect we are. Now, with her so far away, I'm not sure what else to do.

My phone vibrates and I lift it up to see a text from someone I wasn't expecting to hear from.

Fallyn: *Wanna go for a run tomorrow before work?*

Me: *Sure. Meet me at my house at 6 and we'll go.*

Fallyn: *Sounds good =) Night!*

Another Monday morning. I get to the office a little early to get a head start on more paperwork. The run this morning with Fallyn helped clear my head. We didn't talk too much and, surprisingly, the silence between us felt like we had a full-blown conversation. I can't get what she said to me last night out of my head. She's right on so many levels and I should listen to her. Then I think about all the times I've had to push Lisa to remember why we're together. Relationships shouldn't be about always working and fighting to keep the other person happy. If two people are in a relationship and are in love, the rest should fall into place.

My computer pings and dread hits me. Another day full of paperwork, emails, and meetings.

My door slowly opens and Fallyn walks in. "Is this a bad time?"

Quickly checking the time, my jaw nearly drops. It's almost noon and I didn't realize how fast this morning has gone. "Not at all, Fallyn. Have a seat." I put my papers away. "What's going on?"

"Nothing really. I wanted to see how you're doing. You seem so quiet and I'm wondering if you want to head out for the day?"

I look at the time on the computer and then look at her. "You wanna cut out early?"

Her baby blue eyes shine and a smile from ear to ear forms on her face. "Yeah, let's do it. I have Amber covering my shift and I think you and I need to get out now and just be silly. You've been so guarded and I feel bad. You've been helping me work out and I don't really listen to you. I know you and Lisa aren't doing well, so let's head to the bar, grab some food and beer, and talk."

"Alright, game on." I set my automatic response in my email, grab my things, and lead her out of my office. "I've never done this before," I admit.

"Well, there's a first time for everything!"

Chapter 11
Fallyn

After dinner, Isaac heads out on a date while I clean the kitchen. The TV is on and *She's the Man* is playing. If I had someone like Channing Tatum in my life, well, you know what you'd do too. That man is beyond sexy.

Turning off the faucet, I scrub the pots and pans in the sink while watching Mister Oh-So-Sexy on the screen. Finishing with the last pot, I wash my hands and head back to my comfortable couch so I can kick back and finish the movie with a glass of wine in my hand.

The doorbell rings and I curse whoever is on the other side. Opening the door, I raise a brow and look at what he's holding. "Your brother stood me up for someone else. I have sushi," he smirks, pushing himself into my home.

Since meeting Stephen, I think I see him more at my house than anyone else. He and Isaac are close and I like having Stephen around—don't get me wrong—but I also like a nice and quiet house.

Although having him here is nice. He helps me when I need it and we talk about things. I'd consider him a good friend and he's hot. Shit, what am I thinking? Stephen's a friend, just a friend. Right?

"Hungry?" He plops down on the other couch and pulls my coffee table towards him. I cringe as he opens the containers and pays attention to the TV. "Oh I am not watching chick flicks tonight." He grabs the remote from the

Vision of Hope

table and flips through the channels. "Isn't there anything else on tonight?"

"Are you seriously eating in my living room?" I ask him in an annoyed tone. Sitting on the couch beside him I look at the sushi, really wanting some, but deciding against it.

"Ahhh, yeah, sweet cheeks, I am."

"Sweet cheeks?"

"Not a fan of the nickname, huh?" I shake my head. "Okay, what about 'Fal'?"

"Or what about Fallyn because that's my name and I think it's a pretty badass name."

"Badass. That's what your nickname is gonna be."

"Then you'll be S."

"Just S?" I nod. "Fine. Badass and S, BFF?"

"You're a dork. But can I ask you something on a very serious level?"

He chews on the piece of sushi he shoved in his mouth and nods his head, keeping his eyes on me.

"I know you joke around a lot about us dating and you wanting to take me out. Do you mean that? Like you want to?"

He swallows and takes a drink of his beer. "I mean, yeah, I think you're hot and we have fun together. Why are you asking?" He pauses and looks at me. "Are you thinking about dating me?"

"Well, I mean, no. You're my best friend and I love hanging out with you." I sigh. "I was just wondering. Thoughts going through my head."

"You can tell me what's going on with you. I know I'm new to not fucking around with women, but if you want to try and date…"

"No," I cut him off. Thinking about dating scares me. I know Brody isn't coming back, but is it too soon? "A lot happened back in Montana and, I don't know, I was just thinking about what's right and what isn't right."

"If you tell me what's going on, I can try and help you."

Taking the chance to tell Stephen about Brody is weird. I haven't told anyone here about my past. I'm not ashamed of it by any means. It's hard and will always be hard. When you open that piece of your heart to someone else it's normal to feel afraid. I trust Stephen and maybe it'll be a good thing to get a different perspective. Without thinking, I tell him about Brody, the life we had, and his last few moments.

"Damn, girl." He brings me in for a hug. I wipe my tears and smile. It's getting easier to talk about him. I don't know if this means I'm cold hearted or if I don't care about him.

"Thank you for listening. I'm trying to talk about him more. It's hard, but getting easier. Does this mean I'm heartless and I don't care?"

"No. Absolutely not. It means that you're healing. Talking about how you feel is good."

"Yeah." I let out a peaceful sigh. No matter how many days, weeks, months, or years pass, I'll remember Brody and our love. He's the piece of me I'll never let go. He has my heart in Heaven and one day we'll be together, but for now, I'm alive and I need to take advantage of that.

"Thank you for being here for me." I kiss him on the cheek. "You really are my best friend."

"You're mine too." He kisses the side of my head and we get comfortable. I pull a blanket from the top of the couch and lay it across our laps. "What are we watching?"

"No idea," he responds, "Just go with it."

"Okay."

We sit in a comfortable silence and finish the movie. To be honest I have no idea what we watched. "Do you wanna watch something else?" I turn and see Stephen passed out on the couch.

"Night." I kiss his forehead and head to my room.

Vision of Hope

If this were me when I first got to town, I would be freaking out about him staying the night. I'm growing and changing. I like the group of friends I have and I don't mind it when Stephen or anyone else wants to come over and hang out.

Getting comfortable on my bed, I reach over and grip Brody's picture in my hands. Touching his sweet face, admiring him, and missing him. "I told Stephen about you tonight. It felt good. I think it's getting easier and I know that you'd be happy for me that I'm making friends and living my life, but I won't lie, there are days I miss you so much and I'm not sure how I'll get out of bed. I want to move on and be happy, but don't get me wrong; I am happy. There's something missing and I'm not sure what it is. Do you like Stephen?" I pause and let the silence linger in the air. "You know a sign here or there would be nice!"

My phone vibrates on my nightstand. I reach over and unlock my phone. There's a message from Jensen.

Jensen: *Hey. Sorry. I know it's late, but do you know where Stephen is?*

Me: *Yeah, he's at my house. Crashed on the couch. Is everything okay?*

Jensen: *Oh, okay. Awesome. Yeah, everything's good. I was trying to confirm tomorrow with him and make sure he was still good to go.*

Me: *What are you two doing tomorrow?*

Jensen: *Golfing, lol.*

Me: *LOL, nice. Well, have fun! I'm gonna crash. ttyl.*

Jensen: *Good night, Fallyn, and sweet dreams.*

Me: *You too!*

I put my phone back on my nightstand and bring my attention back to Brody. "I'm gonna go to bed. I'll dream of you. I love you so much and I miss you. Every single day."

Kissing his picture, I set it beside me and close my eyes, falling into a deep sleep.

The next few days pass me by. I'm lucky to have two days off in a row. Forty-eight hours without being around patients and feeling the pressures of the hospital sounds incredible.

Finishing the dishes, I press the start button on my dishwasher and feel arms around my waist. I turn and see Stephen resting his chin on my shoulder.

"What?"

"Don't be mad."

I nudge him in the stomach and turn to face him. "Stephen?"

"Isaac and I went halves on a big screen TV. Yours wasn't doing it for us anymore and it'll be here in ten minutes." He bites his hand and his eyes go wide. "Big screen, Badass. Like big."

"What. The. Hell. Did. You. Do."

"Ah, ah, ah. Don't mock it until you see it." I throw my arms in the air and head to sit on the barstool at the island.

"Plus the guys and girls are coming over in about thirty minutes, so there's that."

"Stephen! This is *my* house! You can't just invite people over and buy things. Please consult with me."

He places his hand on my shoulders and rubs the impending tension. "No worries. Relax and have fun today. It's a beautiful day and you should really think about getting an in-ground pool. All the cool kids have it."

"Well, this cool kid can't afford it right now, so there's that." I stick out my tongue at him and he immediately grabs it.

"You aren't a child," he smirks. "So no sticking out your tongue." I swat him away and kick his knee. "Okay, you're a child, so go to your room." We burst out laughing and it feels

Vision of Hope

good to feel alive and normal. Having Stephen around is the best medicine.

Not wanting to stick around with the guys I text Lexi and ask what she's up to.

Lexi: *Come on over! Bring a suit too!*

Grabbing a few things from my room, I tell the boys I'll talk to them later and head out. The drive to Lexi and Larry's is quick. Parking my car I walk around the house and find Lexi and Karly lying on the pool lounges.

"Looks like the two of you are having fun!"

Karly looks up, "You don't even know."

"Where are the kids?"

Lexi answers, "Nicholas and Larry took them so we could have some alone time. My head is killing me. I didn't think being a mom would make me go gray. I don't want to think about when he gets older."

"Try having *two* kids. Don't get me wrong. I love them with my whole heart, but sometimes, just sometimes, I need some me time."

Pulling off my dress I lay down on the other side of Karly and pour myself a glass of Mojito. "Your own concoction?"

"Duh," Lexi says. "And why the hell are you wearing a one piece?" Karly looks over and I look down at my suit. I never was into wearing a bikini. Even though I work out all the time and eat healthy, I still don't like my body. No matter what I do, I'll never be skinny like my two friends.

"What? It's cute!"

"Yeah if you're old and gray," Karly laughs, "Seriously? What's up?"

I take a drink of the Mojito and look at the pool. Placing my glass down, I jump in and feel the coolness of the water on my body. Seriously, maybe I do need to get a pool.

Coming back up I grab a floaty device and lay down. "Nothing to tell," I answer them, "Just like my suit."

S. Moose

This shuts them up for a little and we go back to talking about the kids, their husbands and wanting to take a Vegas trip. For the most part I'm quiet and think about their question. Often I do wonder how I'd look in a bikini. Maybe I'll try one on.

Chapter 12
Lisa

I'm looking up airline tickets and seeing if it's possible to head out this weekend to see Jensen. Between classes and studying I'm finding it impossible to do anything. I mean I could always study with him at his place.

"Ugh," I click out of the site and lay down on my couch. Why does this relationship have to be so hard?

Some of my friends don't understand how I can be with someone so much older or carry a long-distance relationship, but I don't see it that way. I'm lucky to have someone as mature and responsible as Jensen. He has everything together and is successful. What more can I ask for?

Getting up from the couch I go to my room, turn on the music from my iPhone and sit on my bed. I need to take my mind off missing Jensen and get work down. Twirling the diamond heart pendant he got me for my birthday, I lie down on my bed and work on homework. I have a full day of classes tomorrow, along with a huge paper due tomorrow. My phone vibrates on my desk, but it's not who I miss.

Ian: *Dinner?*

Me: *Already ate. I'm fine. I need to work on this paper, though. Ugh.*

Ian's been keeping me company since we ran into each other. We go on lunch and dinner dates and have a morning class together. It's nice to see him again and reconnect.

Ian: *Well, get your work done and come meet us on East tonight. Just one drink.*

Me: *Fine! ONE drink!*

* * * * *

My alarm blares and I slowly open my eyes. My mind is foggy and I can't remember how the hell I made it home last night. Slowly getting up, I notice there are guy clothes all over the bedroom floor. Pushing myself up on the bed, I look over and see Ian lying next to me. "Fuck!" He's naked and I'm naked. "No! No!" Brushing my hand through my hair, I try and think about last night. It was just *one* drink! But then it comes back to me. One drink led to a few shots, which led to another drink and some more shots.

This isn't happening. I didn't cheat on Jensen. I love Jensen. He's my world, but here I am and, fuck, what the hell am I going to do?

Pushing Ian off my bed, I throw his clothes at him and scream for him to get out. "Ian, you need to leave now! Seriously! I can't believe this happened!"

"Whoa," he says, putting on his boxers. "Can we at least talk?"

"Talk? Talk! About what? That I got insanely drunk last night and then we had sex and I have a boyfriend! A boyfriend who I love very much."

Ian doesn't respond. He stares at me, looks away, and then walks around the bed and comes to stand in front of me. Tilting my head up with his finger, he lightly kisses my lips. "Everything happens for a reason," he whispers before kissing me again. There's passion and longing in his kiss. My hands are in his hair, holding him closer to me.

"Ian," I breathlessly say, resting my forehead against his. "We can't do this. I love Jensen."

"But you love me too."

"What?"

Hands caress my face. Feather kisses all over me as he wraps his arms around me, resting his chin on top of my head. "I never let you go. You came here for a reason. Everything that's happened has led us to this point. I know you're in a shitty position and, normally, I'd leave, since you have a boyfriend, but you're not fighting me on this. I know you want this just as much as I do." I nod my head. "See? We're perfect together."

"So are me and Jensen." Saying his name is killing me. How could I have done this to him? The plans we had and everything we've talked about is out the window. My chest tightens and tears form in my eyes. Having Ian back means the world to me. We left with so many unanswered questions, and now he's back, but I have someone who loves me and will do anything for me. I can't do this to either of them. But my heart is screaming not to let Ian go.

"I need time to think." I sigh, pushing away from him. On my wall, there are pictures of me and Jensen. Pictures of our love and time together. He spent hours creating this wall for me when I first moved in.

In the middle, there's a picture of us at dinner. His arm is resting on my shoulders, and we're both smiling. There are lilies in the middle of the table. The dinner was a "just because" dinner because he wanted to spend time with me. The surrounding pictures are of us doing various things from spending time on the beach back in Wilmington to driving in his car, or just us being lazy and hanging out.

"I know I came back and things aren't what they're supposed to be, but I'll make you realize how good we are together." Ian kisses my cheek and walks out of my room.

My bedroom is quiet and I'm alone to think about the things I've done and the mess I've made. Picking up my phone, I send a text to Jensen.

Me: *I miss you...Can you please come see me soon?*

My Love: *What's wrong??*

Me: *I'm just having a hard time adjusting here alone and I've been in a bad place for the past few hours. I don't know what to do anymore.*

My Love: *Baby, don't give up. You can do this. I know it's hard and you feel like the world is crumbling down on you, but all this hard work will pay off. You're talented, smart, and have a lot to offer the medical world. Don't give up, okay? I'm here for you, no matter what. I wish I could drop everything and be with you. I wish we could have that, but, baby, all good things come to those who wait. I believe that this is the test of our relationship. If we can get through this, we can get through anything. Don't worry about making mistakes. Whatever you do, I'm here for you and support you 100%.*

Me: *You don't know how badly I needed to hear you say that to me.*

My Love: *Anytime you need me or anything, you know I'm here, Lisa. I'll always be here for you. Your biggest fan and supporter, baby. I love you.*

Me: *I love you too.*

As I press send, the tears I've been holding back release from my eyes. The emotions drain out of me and I feel weak. So weak. I can't grasp my life and what I did. I can't see straight. Things are going out of control and I have no idea what to do.

Me: *I need you to come see me, please. I need my big brother =(*

I spend the day in bed and don't get out. I turned off my phone once Stephen said he'd get on the next flight to come see me. He'll know what to do.

By midnight, I hear the front door open. I've been wide awake, afraid to fall asleep. Because when I close my eyes, I see Ian and Jensen. Both men that I want and love. Both men that I'm destroying by the lies and deception.

"Lisa?" Stephen comes in and sits on the side of my bed. "What's going on?"

Since our parents died, Stephen's been the only constant in my life, before Jensen. He's been there for me through all the ups and downs. He's been my big brother, mom, and dad. We were left with a big inheritance from my parents and he's been taking care of everything, since I was too young to realize what was going on. Stephen's eight years older, so when we lost our parents when I was fourteen, he became my guardian and made sure I was okay. Everything I am and everything I've learned has been because of Stephen's love. I'm so afraid to disappoint him and a part of me doesn't know what to do. If I tell him, then he'll know and he'll feel the need to tell Jensen. I can't have him do that. I can't have Jensen find out, not now, at least.

"Stephen, I messed up so bad," I cry, resting my head on his lap. "I don't know what to do."

"What happened?"

"I don't know," I murmur in a soft voice. "I don't know where to begin, but you're going to hate me. You're going to hate me so much."

"Sweetheart, whatever you tell me won't make me hate you."

"I cheated on Jensen," I sigh, burying my face away from the reality that I'm facing. Maybe if I close my eyes, everything will be fine, and what I did will never have happened. But when I feel Stephen's body tense, his hands balling in fists, I know that I'm about to feel even worse.

"With who?"

"Ian," I quietly respond. "I don't know what I'm going to do," I sob, hugging his leg, not wanting him to leave. "What am I going to do?"

Stephen doesn't say anything. I'm afraid to look at him. I'm afraid to see his expression. How did my life get this fucked up in a matter of a day?

"I can't believe you!" he screams, getting off the bed. "Jensen's the best thing that's happened to you. Do you know how much he loves you, Lisa?"

"I know!" I scream back, sitting on my bed. My hands are in my hair as I sob uncontrollably. "Okay, I know that I fucked up! But how do I solve this? What do I do?"

"You need to tell him, Lisa. You can't fucking hide this shit. Seriously, you told me and expect me to keep this from him? He's my Goddamn best friend."

"And I'm your fucking sister! You need to help me, Stephen."

He shakes his head. "I don't know how, Lisa. Yes, you are my sister and I love you very much, but, sweetheart, this is a mistake that you need to handle. This is your life and you need to figure it out. You can't be selfish. If you don't love Jensen, then let him go."

"I'm going crazy with the distance between us. It's so hard and unfair."

"That's life, Lisa. Life is unfair. It brings us down when we're at the highest point and stomps on our heart. But you can't let it define you. You need to rise above the shit you've done and deal with it head on. It won't go away."

I nod, not knowing what to say.

I'll make it go away. If I don't think about it or talk about it, then it never happened.

Chapter 13
Jensen

Pulling into the Fallyn's driveway, I get out of my car and knock on her front door. It's been two days since she found out about the death of Eric. It's hard on her and I can understand. There's nothing she could have done and I hate that she's blaming herself. That's one of the major downfalls with getting into medicine, the risk of losing your patients. The support system from the hospital has been great and the nurses have been coming to sit with Fallyn, but she's still upset. I can't imagine how she's feeling.

The door opens and she looks up at me. Her blue eyes are full of sadness, and dark circles invade her face. Dressed in only sweatpants and a t-shirt, she opens the door for me, walking back to the couch and sitting down. There are tissues all over her living room floor. Sitting down next to her, I hand her flowers, hoping to see her smile.

"Thanks," she mutters, taking the flowers and setting them on the table.

"Feeling better?" She shrugs. "You know this isn't your fault."

"I know." She wipes her nose, still hugging her knees against her body. "It's still hard, though. I've been with Eric for months and he was so special to me. I don't know what to do. His mom is a mess and everyone on the floor is so sad. He was so young."

"I know and it sucks. I wish I had magic words to make you feel better, but I don't. The best thing I can tell you is how lucky Eric was to have you. Lucy talked highly of you and appreciated you for being his nurse. See, Fallyn? You're making a huge difference in these kids' lives and sometimes, yeah, you're going to experience death, but look at the positives. These kids are getting love and care from *you* and the whole department. We're giving them a fighting chance. You may lose a few battles, but the war of being a nurse, you'll never lose."

She rests her head on my shoulder and blows her nose. "Thanks, Jensen."

"You're welcome."

We sit like this for a few moments. I look around her house. It's small but homey. There isn't a table, but instead an island with four barstools. The living room holds a loveseat and a sectional. There are pictures all over her walls, but one catches my eye.

"Who is that?" I ask, looking at Fallyn. Her face goes pale and she starts biting her lower lip. She walks over to the picture and stares at it for a few moments. I'm not sure if I should say something or change the topic.

"That's Brody. I haven't really been able to talk about him, besides to Isaac and Stephen. I put up his picture yesterday. Since being here, I never thought about it. For some reason, I thought it would be okay to put up his picture and let people in, you know?" I nod, and she turns around to face me. "It's been a weird few weeks. But when I put up his picture, I don't know I felt better I guess." She's pacing the living room and then stops by the window leaning against the wall. "Life is so short. We never know what's going to happen or if we'll see tomorrow. See, Brody was taken from me," she quietly explains, breathing in and out, trying to remain calm. "His ex-girlfriend came over to talk to him. Well, let me backtrack; Brody and I started dating when we were sixteen. We broke up when we were twenty and he dated this girl named Kristen.

Vision of Hope

I was so heartbroken, but after like three months, he broke up with her and came back to me. He said that being with her, there was nothing. He wanted to see what it would be like to date other girls. I didn't take him back right away. I made him fight for me, and he did. When we got back together, it was great, and he proposed to me a few months later. So yeah, Kristen came over to our house and wanted to talk to Brody. She wanted him back and couldn't let him go. Crazy right?" She stops talking and I don't dare interrupt her. Leaning forward with my forearms on my thighs, I watch her as she paces the room.

"She shot him, and then shot herself when she thought she killed him. When I came home after getting my wedding dress, I found him. He died in my arms."

Her body shakes and her face turns pale. I quickly get up and bring her in my arms. "I'm so sorry, Fallyn."

Her eyes immediately meet mine and tears spring out. I feel like an asshole. Placing my arm around hers, I bring her to me and let her cry.

"It's been a little over six months and I want to move on and be happy. I can't. I feel guilty feeling this way, like I'm not honoring his memory and who he was."

"It takes time to get over the death of someone you love." Fallyn nods her head. "You have every right to grieve, but don't allow your grief to stop you from doing what you love."

We sit in silence and I think this is what she needs—a place where it's quiet, but she's not alone. Her head rests on the pillow while she lies on the couch. I'm working on the laptop at her kitchen table, reviewing medical records and files. I look over and she hasn't moved in the past few hours. Hearing my stomach grumble, I turn off my laptop and walk over to Fallyn. Kneeling down beside her, I brush a strand of hair from her face.

"Why don't I take you to get something to eat?"

"Not hungry."

Nodding my head to the door, I say, "Come on, Fallyn. My treat. Even if we walk outside, it's something you need to do. You can't be trapped in your house."

"I wanna be alone." She closes her eyes, letting out a shaky breath.

"Well, I'm not going to let you be alone." I smirk. "Come on; let's go, and I'll let you pay for me."

She laughs. Finally, a smile or some sort of emotion resembling happiness. "Thanks, Jensen." She offers me a small smile, placing her hand on my arm. "I am hungry, though."

I pull her from the couch, and we head out and get food. Heading a few blocks from her house, we walk to a quiet diner and take the booth in the back. My phone vibrates in my pocket, but I ignore it.

The server greets us and hands us menus. "I'll be back in a few moments, folks. Take your time."

"Thanks." Looking through the menu, I settle on ordering a BLT sandwich with fries and extra pickles. I love pickles, but Lisa hates them and hates it when I order pickles because she says it makes my breath smell. I smile, thinking about her.

"Thinking about Lisa?"

"Yeah, and it sucks. She's pissed at me, as usual. I need her to focus on school and not so much on our relationship. She doesn't understand how hard this program at Fisher is. If she can't handle the heat now, I don't know how she'll handle being a nurse in a hospital."

"But you can't blame her for missing you. It's normal, Jensen. Be sure you're letting her know how much you love her and miss her."

"I do, but whatever. I'm going to let her throw this tantrum. Honestly, it's getting exhausting. Can we talk about something else, please?"

Vision of Hope

"Okay, so this question is going to sound weird, but I saw a picture of you and Emma at Karly's house. You're her uncle?"

"Ah, yeah. Karly's my best friend."

"She looks so much like you." Grabbing my water, I take a few gulps. This isn't a story I like to tell.

"How did you meet everyone?"

"I don't know. I moved here and met Karly. And here we are."

She eyes me slowly. "You're hiding something from me."

"I'm not."

"You definitely are. Tell me!"

I kink my brows together. Shit. "Well, it's a long and complicated story."

"Go on! Seriously, I wanna know!"

"Fine." I hesitate and then tell her about the colossal mess Jamie left and the history between all of us. Her eyes grow wide. She covers her mouth with her tiny hands and shakes her head. "And now here we are."

"Whoa, that's crazy."

"You're telling me. Emma has no idea and that's what we want. I love her enough not to destroy her life. She's only known Nicholas as her dad and I don't want to ruin that for her because Jamie messed up."

Hands go up to her mouth as she shakes her head and her body shakes. Why the hell do women do this? It's not that interesting. "Holy crap! That's some crazy drama. You guys should all get your own reality show!" She leans back, crossing her arms over her chest. I try not to stare at her. There's a pull to Fallyn I can't explain. It's captivating to see her getting lost in her thoughts and looking relaxed. Sometimes, I wish I could get lost in my thoughts and not worry about the things that are going on in my life.

We sit in silence, but in my head, there's loud noise and voices.

She's beautiful sitting across from me, looking out the window. I can talk to her about everything and she doesn't judge or turn it around so that the situation connects to her.

Fuck, this isn't good.

"Thanks for listening to me and being here. You're a really great friend and it means a lot to me." She smiles.

"I'm glad you're smiling and laughing. I like hanging out with you and consider you a good friend. Whenever you need to talk or anything just let me know." The waitress comes back and we put in our orders.

After we're done eating, part of me doesn't want to say goodbye. Looking over at her, I notice her shoulders are a bit slumped and there's still that distant look in her eyes. I know this doesn't look good and I should go home and talk to Lisa. My girlfriend Lisa. The woman I love and the woman I want to spend my life with.

Then again, she's upset and we're friends. I want to be here for her so she doesn't feel alone.

"Where's Isaac tonight?"

"He left to go see his parents in Montana for a few weeks."

"You okay with being alone?"

There's no answer from her. I wait a few minutes before I talk about something else. It's obvious this topic isn't her favorite.

"I hate being alone. When I'm alone, I find myself talking to Brody's picture. I'm crazy or can't move on. I just feel closer to him and it's nice to see him. Is that crazy?"

"No. Not at all." I place my arm around her shoulders and kiss the side of her head.

Chapter 14
Fallyn

Going out with Jensen doesn't make me feel uneasy. But walking next to him, down the quiet road, seems too familiar. For the first time since losing Brody, I feel good. For so long, I've wanted to be with a man and feel what it's like to be in love and feel a man's touch on my body. I put others before me, especially my job, and haven't been able to let myself go. With the guilt from Brody's death still looming, I have to keep busy so I don't lose my mind thinking about the possibilities.

It's hard not to think about all of that when I'm with Jensen. I've been laughing and smiling more. Sure, I've been happy around Stephen, but Jensen's a different feeling. He's a different kind of happy, if that makes sense. This type of happy can lead to a crush, which can lead to me falling for him.

I smile again, thinking about the possibility of falling for him. Then reality hits me in the face. I cannot fall for him. It's not right and he has a girlfriend. I've been helping him with his relationship! What the hell is wrong with me?

"Sorry, Fallyn. Excuse me. Lisa's calling."

Lisa. His girlfriend. The woman he loves.

We're friends and friends hang out. He's like a Stephen. He has to be in the same category as Stephen. But why am I upset? Why do I care that he has a girlfriend? It's not like I like him or anything. I'm not supposed to like someone who is in a committed relationship. It's wrong on all levels.

Distancing myself from Jensen is the only way I can protect myself and their relationship.

He's a few feet back from me, talking on the phone, and he's smiling. It's a happy relationship. Continuing my walk to my house, I take out my phone to see how Isaac's doing.

Isaac: *I'll be home soon. I know you miss me and you're having a hard time. Mom is sick and Dad's out of town.*

Me: *No, I'll be okay. I'm a big girl. Please tell her to feel better and send my love.*

Isaac: *You know if you need me to come home, I will. In a heartbeat.*

Having Isaac right now by my side is what I need.

Me: *I'll be okay! Take care of her and I'll ttyl.*

Isaac: *K, love you.*

Me: *Love you too.*

Opening my front door, I peek behind me to see if Jensen is coming. I don't see him, so I close the door and head to my bedroom. I know I shouldn't be upset or angry. I have no right to be. We had something to eat and walked and talked. There's nothing romantic about it.

I push down my feelings and curl up in bed, where I've been for the past two days. My phone vibrates from under my pillow. When I swipe to unlock my phone, I see that it's a text from Jensen.

Jensen: *Hey, where'd you go? Sorry about that. Lisa called and I needed to talk to her.*

I don't respond.

Jensen: *Fallyn? Well, I'm coming back to your house, so hopefully, you're here.*

Damn.

Me: *Thank you for having dinner with me. I'm tired and have a headache. I'll see you later.*

Jensen: *All right. Are you sure?*

Me: *Positive.*

Vision of Hope

He doesn't respond and it bothers me. Pulling the pillow under my head, I scream a few times, cursing myself for these emotions.

The next few days, I find myself avoiding Jensen at all costs. I miss running outside and I miss my morning shifts at the hospital. I've been working the swing shift so I can avoid him and sleep the morning and afternoon away. He's been texting me, asking how I'm doing, and if I want to go for a run. I text him back with the usual responses.

I'm tired.

Overnight again.

Maybe next time.

These are the only responses I can come up with. Hopefully he'll get the hint and leave me alone. I'm not trying to be a bitch or anything. It's getting too close to comfort and I don't want anyone getting the wrong idea.

Sitting in the living room with Isaac and Stephen, watching *Insidious,* I want to curl up in a ball and die. I have no idea why I agreed to watch this awful movie with them. The living room is dark and the curtains are closed. The only light in the room is coming from the TV. If I die tonight, at least it'll be quick.

"Are you scared?"

I turn and swat Stephen away. I've been covering my eyes for the majority of the movie. I have no idea what's going on except for weird things happening and people dying in a gruesome way.

"Feel like cuddling?" He raises both brows. I slap him again. "Stop hitting me. That turns me on."

"You're such a pig. Why are you here anyways?"

"I wanted to spend quality time with my second best girl and my bromance."

"Second best girl?" I repeat back to him.

Stephen cocks his head to the side. "Yep. My first best girl would be Leslie. She's my girlfriend." He winks. "I listened to your advice and we talked. Taking things slow, but she's awesome."

Did I hear him right? Stephen actually has a girlfriend?

"She's pretty hot," Isaac adds. "And can cook."

"The both of you suck so much right now!" I huff, grabbing my blanket to go back to my room. Pulling out my Kindle, I click on my next read and get comfortable on my papasan. A few minutes later, there's a knock on my door.

"Stephen, leave me alone!"

The door opens and in walks Jensen. "Hey." He raises his hand, walks in, and sits on the bedroom floor in front of me.

"Hi. What are you doing here?"

"You've been avoiding me and I want to know why."

I sigh. "I don't know. I've been working the swing shift and I'm tired."

"But you have Stephen in your living room."

"He came over to hang out with Isaac and they wanted to watch a movie. Notice how I'm in my room."

"So you didn't go out there with them."

I bite my nail. "Well, I tried watching the movie until Stephen got annoying, so I left and came in here."

"Why are you avoiding me?"

Because I don't want to fall for you. "I really haven't been."

He points at me. "You're lying. Seriously, be straight with me. What's going on?"

"Seriously! Nothing. I've been busy. You're being really annoying and I don't know what else I have to say to get you to believe that I'm fine and I've been working a lot lately."

"All right. Fine. I believe you. Do you wanna grab a drink and food?"

"No, I'm heading to bed. I have a sixteen-hour shift tomorrow." I shut off my Kindle and get up to walk Jensen out from my room. "I'll talk to you later."

"Have a good night, Fallyn." He squeezes my hand, smiles, and walks away.

Damn you, Jensen. Damn you.

Chapter 15
Jensen

"HI!" Karly waves her hand in my face. "Best friend here wanting to talk to her best friend, but he's ignoring her!"

"Sorry, sweetheart." I smile, picking at the food in front of me. It's Thursday night and I've been racking my brain, trying to figure out what's going on with Lisa and Fallyn. It's been over a week and they've been distant. I shouldn't care about Fallyn being distant. She made it clear that she's been busy with work. It bothers me that we went from having easy conversations and hanging out to barely talking to one another.

"What's wrong?" She pouts, picking up her wine glass and taking a sip.

"I don't know," I grumble, trying not to be a complete douchebag. Karly and I get together as much as we can and talk. She's been there for me since I came to Wilmington and has forgiven me for what I've done to her and her family. I'm lucky to have her as my best friend and someone who accepts me and my faults. "Lisa's been acting weird and Fallyn's avoiding me."

"Why?"

"That's the thing. I have no idea. Lisa barely texts me back and, when she does, it's simple responses. I'll text her and wish her a great day and that I'm thinking about her and love her, but I get nothing back from her. Every time I call her, I get her voicemail. She's been online too. I see her Facebook updates, so I'm not fucking dumb. And Fallyn's been picking up these overnight shifts."

"She wants to work so she doesn't let her mind wander. That's all normal, well, minus Lisa. But the thing with Fallyn, don't sweat it. Wait; why are you sweating it?"

"No reason. She's a friend and I like hanging out with her."

"Right. Okay, so that's cool. Now, about Lisa. She's in school, and you said it yourself that she's busy with classes. I mean, science and bio and all that stuff is hard." I raise a brow at her, taking in everything she's said. "Okay, so she's on Facebook and not talking to you. I wouldn't worry. You worry too much."

"Thanks, *Stephen.*"

"Hey, don't get mad at me because we gave you advice that you don't like." She pauses, taking another sip of her wine. "I think you're worried about nothing. Just keep trying with Lisa and understand where she's coming from. You need to talk to her and stop fighting. Both of you are so stubborn!"."

I see Karly grinning before me, shake my head, and immediately change the topic. "So tell me more about Emma and Sebastian."

* * * * *

Another day in the office. I check my phone and there's still nothing from Lisa. I texted her a few times this morning with no response. She's busy with classes—I get it—but a message back wouldn't hurt.

My computer beeps, letting me know I have a meeting in fifteen minutes. I grab the files needed along with my phone and coffee. When I leave my office, I hear Fallyn calling my name.

"Morning." She hands me a bag.

"Morning. What's this?" I look inside and the smell of pumpkin hits my nose. "Thank you!" I excitedly say. I love pumpkin anything.

"You're welcome! I made it this morning after my workout."

"Why didn't you tell me? I would've met up with you."

"I know and I'm sorry. Honestly, it was a quick workout because my knee started bothering me."

"What happened?"

"Sports injury. It was my freshman year and ugh." She shakes her head. "I was about to score and *bam*! Everything got dark, and the next thing I knew, I was in the hospital. The doctor said that, with my injury, it was best to stop playing. I cried for months. Soccer was my *life*."

"I'm sorry about that."

"It's all right! Live and learn, yeah?"

"Yeah." I laugh, holding the door for her as we both walk into the conference room. During the meeting, my mind is reeling. She's been avoiding me and now, today, she's bringing me breakfast and sitting next to me during the meeting. Maybe Karly's right and I'm overreacting.

Hanging out with Fallyn is different. When we hang out, I don't have too many worries on my mind. It scares me how relaxed I am with her. I'm not sure if it's because our friendship is new or if there's something else going on. Being with her helps and I don't want to lose that connection.

On a piece of paper, I write her a note.

I miss our talks and hanging out. I want my friend back, please.

I slide her the note, still keeping my eyes on the presentation. She takes it from beneath my fingers and, in a few moments, slides back her response.

I miss hanging out too. Wanna go for a run tonight?

Yes, please.

The meeting lets out after a few hours. It's been a long day and I'm ready to head home. Karly texted me earlier and told me to come over for family night. Not sure when this started, but she wants all of us over to hang out. It'll be nice to see everyone and not be locked in my office. Looking over the last few emails, I then log out of Outlook and shut down my computer. After making sure my cabinets are locked, I head out of the office and see Fallyn walking in my direction.

"Wow, you're getting out on time?" I laugh, nudging her arm.

"I have to be in at five tomorrow morning," she whines, pushing her hands back through her hair. "I'm exhausted and all I want is my bed, but Karly wants me to come over tonight."

"So come hang out."

"What about our run?"

"Let's do that now and then we'll head out to Karly's."

"I'll think about it."

"If you don't, then Karly's going to be pissed, and I'll be hurt that we missed a run." I know she won't, but I want her to come over tonight and have fun with us. "Please?"

She rolls her eyes and scoffs, "Fine. What should I bring?"

As if on cue, my phone vibrates and a text from Karly comes in. I open the message and show Fallyn.

Karly: *Don't forget my peanut butter chocolate ice cream =)*

"Got it! See you in a little."

I wave goodbye and walk to my car. Getting in, I send Lisa a text, knowing it'll go unanswered like every text I've sent her lately.

Me: *I miss you.*

* * * * *

S. Moose

I pull up to Nicholas and Karly's house with a pack of beer for the guys. I enjoy nights like this with my friends. Not only do I get to let loose a little, but I get to spend some time with Emma. With my busy schedule, it's hard to spend time with her. I've been trying to take her out at least once a week, but I'm a few weeks short. I know she's in good hands with Nicholas and Karly, and I think that's another reason why I'm okay with them raising my beautiful little girl.

As I ring the doorbell, I hear laughter on the other side. My girl opens the door with the biggest smile on her face. I kneel down and hand her a bouquet of wild flowers.

"Thank you, Uncle Jensen." She throws her little arms around my neck and I carry her inside.

"You're welcome, Angel. How are you today?"

"Good. Mommy said that you might be coming to my show next week?"

"I'm going to try my hardest." As I walk in the kitchen, I see Karly, Lexi, and Fallyn around the island, laughing and drinking wine. The guys are in the living room and Stephen's outside on the deck on the phone. I put Emma down, kiss the girls on the cheek, and say hi to Fallyn. I head outside to check on Stephen.

"You need to talk to him. Stop playing these games. If you don't want to be with him, then call if off!" he screams. I have a feeling I know what's going on. "I gotta go," he says when he sees me sitting down.

"Was that Lisa?" Stephen nods, joining me and taking a beer from my hand. "What the hell does your sister want?"

Stephen sighs. "All I can say is talk to her and go see her, man. I don't know if you want to hear this from me. You're my best friend and I love you, man, but this is something you and her have to figure out together."

"Fuck," I groan.

Chapter 16
Fallyn

Running today with Jensen and spending time with him is messing with my head. I shouldn't care about him or think about him. I shouldn't want his lips on mine. When we're together, I don't think about Brody and the pain in my heart isn't there.

Does that make me a bad person?

Of course it does. Of course, it makes me an *awful* person. Here I am falling for my friend who has a girlfriend. A girlfriend he truly loves. I don't want to get in the way of his relationship. I'm still mourning Brody. It hasn't been a year, so I shouldn't be thinking about another man or moving on.

My mind goes back to the shadows. Thinking about Brody is like a knife to my heart. I'm trying to get on with my life and doing what I love to do. I don't feel guilty for leaving because this was the plan. Brody is always on my mind and my heart will always be broken without him. But I think back to Beth's words, about moving on with my life and finding happiness. I think back to Jensen's words about moving on. It hasn't come across my mind until now. My focus has been on my patients and work.

"So Nicholas thought he was being romantic and sexy when he was doing his sexy dance." Karly laughs and snorts, trying to hold her wine. "And then Emma...Emma walked in and Nicholas ran to the bathroom. Needless to say, we didn't do anything."

"Baby, really?" Nicholas yells from the living room.

"Oh, that's nothing! Larry and I haven't been doing much of anything because of Kayden."

"Little man's a cock blocker!"

Lexi shakes her head. "It's true. I haven't had a *real* orgasm in *forever*. Karly, I have no idea how you do it with Emma and Sebastian."

Karly shrugs and drinks her wine. "Honestly, we've just been having quickies. Don't get me wrong, it's great. I miss the hour-long sex sessions, though. Like the foreplay to actually having sex. Do you know how bad I miss his tongue on me?"

"Baby!"

"Oh, you're fine." She waves him off. "It's like a wham, bam, I love you thing. But it gets the job done. Seriously, Lex, just try it. All you need is," Karly pauses and thinks, "three minutes, tops."

Larry bursts out laughing and Nicholas comes to the kitchen, pulling his wife to his side. "First, it's not three minutes and, second, I can last longer if I want."

She pats his arm. "It's okay, baby. You're more than enough for me."

Lexi shakes her head. "Ew, gross images."

I watch the room erupt with laughter. There's a small ache in my heart. It's these moments that make me miss my past. I imagine Brody sitting in the living room with the guys, drinking a beer, and laughing along with everyone else.

"Hey, why are Jensen and Stephen outside?" Lexi asks, and we all look towards the deck.

"Not sure. I'll go check."

When Karly walks away and goes outside, Lexi drinks more of her wine and sighs. "What's wrong?" I ask Lexi.

"Oh." She puts down her wine glass. "Just weird things. Everyone's been acting weird lately, especially Stephen. He's distant. No idea what's going on with him. You've been hanging with him, though. Has he said anything?"

"No. He hasn't said anything. I know he went to see Lisa, but when he came back, he kept blowing Isaac off and saying he has to work. Could that be it?"

Lexi takes my hand and we make our way to the living room. She sits next to Larry and I sit on the other side of Nicholas. I'm not sure what the men of Wilmington do or drink, but damn, they are sexy. I sip my white wine and look around the living room. It's full of pictures of Nicholas, Karly, their kids, family, and friends.

"Karly's obsessed with capturing every moment she can," Nicholas says, leaning in to closer. "Decorating the house is her specialty." He looks at me, then at the pictures, and points at the large picture above the fireplace. "That was taken in Hawaii back in July. It was my thirtieth and Emma's sixth birthday."

Looking at the picture, I can't help to feel a little jealous. Even though I'm young and still have time to eventually have a family, it hurts knowing the one man I wanted to spend my life with and have a family with will never happen. I look at the smiles on their face and how happy they are. It's a great feeling to see your friends happy, but it sucks knowing you won't get that any time soon. "You have a beautiful family, Nicholas."

"Thanks. Karly told me that she's trying to set you up with someone, so if you need help, let me know."

"No! No." I laugh uneasily. "I'm not ready to date. It's so hard balancing life and work. Right now, I'm perfectly happy spending time with you guys and the kids."

"Understandable."

Nicholas and I talk about basketball and the hospital some more before Stephen, Jensen, and Karly come back to the living room.

"You doing okay?" Jensen asks, taking a seat on the floor, resting his back on my leg.

"Awesome. Tonight's been so fun."

The guys watch the fight on TV while me, Lexi, and Karly head back to the kitchen and sit at the table, talking about life and their husbands. Playing with the wine glass in my hands, I listen like a good friend should, but my attention is on the very sexy man out in the living room. It's clear that he's off limits, yet he's igniting my body and my broken heart.

"What's going on?" I look up and see Karly looking at me. "You've been so quiet. Are you okay?"

I'd rather not discuss the thoughts in my head. "Honestly, I'm getting tired. I have to be at work by five a.m., and work sixteen hours."

It's as if Jensen has powers because, when I tell them I'm tired, he's by my side, asking if I want to leave.

"You can stay," I inform him.

"No, I should get going too. I'll follow you home."

Don't think anything about this. He's just being nice.

* * * * *

It's been a long night and I'm not looking forward to another sixteen-hour shift tomorrow. I lock my car and see Jensen walking over to me.

"Can I come in, Fallyn?"

I look at Jensen and cock my head to the side. "Jensen, it's late. Thank you for following me back home, but it wasn't necessary. I mean, what are you doing?"

"I don't know," he whispers. "I wanted to make sure you got home okay."

There's a pull I'm feeling to Jensen. I push back, though. Whatever feelings I have for him can't surface. It's never a good idea to fall for your boss slash friend slash man with a girlfriend. It's a deadly combination and someone will end up hurt. Even if I can't stop looking in his eyes or wonder how he kisses. "Well, I am. I'm fine." I muster a smile and turn to walk to my door. When I turn around, Jensen's standing in the same spot with his hands in his pockets. "Good night. I'll talk to you later."

"Can we go for a run tomorrow night? I like running with you."

I nod. "Yeah, we can do that. Get home safely."

I don't wait for him to respond. I open my front door, walk inside, and close the door. Turning the lock, I peek out of the window and he's still standing there, looking at me, watching me. I'm not sure how I should feel. I'm not sure if I'm scared.

The next evening, Jensen meets me at my house, ready to go for our run. Grabbing my things from the counter we head outside and stretch for a few minutes.

"Doing okay?" I ask him.

"Yeah. Same old," he forces a laugh, "Maybe this run will be good. Need to clear my head."

Both of us have our ear buds in and give each other thumbs up before we start running. That's what we usually do when we're running since neither of us really talk. We run side by side and go until it's time to turn around. I don't know how to explain it fully. We're in sync when we run and know what to do. I guess we're used to this, since we've been running together for a while.

I want to ask him about Lisa and see if they're doing better. He seems to be okay and I'm glad. But why does my heart wildly beat in my chest when I see him?

When I turn my head, I see that Jensen's not next to me. I stop running and turn around. He's looking down at his phone and has a puzzled expression.

"What's wrong?"

"Can we go back to your house, please?"

"Yeah, we can, but what's wrong?"

He doesn't respond. Instead of answering my questions, he takes off running and I'm right behind him. We're back at my house and I get him situated in the kitchen. Needing a shower, I let Jensen know I'll be back.

Running up the stairs and to my bathroom, I jump in the shower and wash quickly. Drying off, I put on yoga pants and a tank top. Rushing back downstairs, I notice Jensen resting on my couch. I sit opposite of him and wait for him to talk. His eyes look heavy and he's deep in thought.

"I want to believe Lisa and I will be okay. I want to believe this is a test that we have to pass and, once we do, everything will be okay."

"You lost me. What's going on?"

"Stephen texted me. He said I need to go see her soon and that I shouldn't keep putting it off. I texted Lisa, but she hasn't said anything. So when I texted back Stephen, he said that he loves me like a brother and doesn't want to see me hurt. He said that Lisa's going through a lot and I should be there and help her and let her know that I'm here."

"Which I've told you."

"Yeah, well, I'm tired of it. I'm tired of having to show her how much I love her. Why can't she realize that she means so much to me? You know, when she was here, everything was great. She's awesome and I connect with her, but fuck, she's making it hard to fight."

I don't respond. I'm not sure what to say. So I sit back and let him vent.

"I want peace. I want a family and to settle down. Is that too much to ask for?"

I scoot over and by the way he's breathing and shaking his head, I'm not sure if he wants me to get closer. So I scoot a little closer each time. He doesn't say anything. When I'm right next to him, I place my arm around his shoulder and let him know that I'm here without saying the words.

Chapter 17
Lisa

I sit here on my couch. The curtains are drawn and I haven't changed in three days. At this moment, now, I hate life. I hate myself. I can't believe I cheated on Jensen and he's supposed to be here in a few days.

Ian's been trying to get a hold of me, but I haven't responded. Talking to Ian isn't going to do anything for me but cause confusion. When we were together, I felt something for him. How can I love both Ian and Jensen? Is it possible?

I look at my phone and look at Jensen's name. I see his bright eyes and his smile. Everything about him is perfect, but I did the unthinkable and now I have to live with it.

Pushing myself up from the couch, I head to the kitchen and grab a bottle of water. There's a knock on my door and I think about not answering it, but decide against it. When I open the door, I see Ian on the other side, holding three bags of takeout.

"I didn't know if you wanted Chinese or Indian, so I got both."

"Ian, what are you doing here?"

He tries to come in, but I don't open the door to let him in. "I want to be here for you. I know what we did is messed up, but I can't stop thinking about you. I believe in fate and everything happens for a reason, Lisa. You're here for a reason, same as me. Let me in, please."

I let him in and we both sit in my living room. I can't look at him. This shouldn't be happening, but I want it to.

Something inside me is yelling to see what Ian's looking for and to get the answers. I know it's wrong, but Jensen isn't here when I need him. He's putting his job before me and our relationship. If he can be selfish, so can I. I don't care what Stephen says or anyone else. This is my life and my choice to be here with Ian. Plus, it's not like Jensen will find out.

"I don't know what you want me to say, Ian. I'm with Jensen," I start to say, looking at my hands. "I'm happy and my life with him makes sense, but so do you. How can I do this? Why did we break up in the first place?"

"You know," he sits down on the couch, looking at his hands. "I've been thinking about that since I saw you. I don't know why we broke up. I don't know why we lost touch, but I do know that you're here and this has to be my second chance. I know you're with someone else and I hate being the other man." Ian gets up and walks over to me. He places his hands on my shoulders. "But I can't help it. I want you, Lisa. You're all I've been thinking about. Walking away from you for the second time was the hardest thing to do. I gave you space so you could think about what you want and I know you're still confused." He kisses my forehead and rubs my shoulders. "Let me help you make this clear. You love me still, right?" I nod my head. "And you know I love you. No other woman compares to you."

"How can we do this? Do I break up with Jensen?"

Ian kisses me again and invades my mouth with his tongue. His hands are in my hair and little moans are leaving my lips. "Let's see where it goes," he whispers against my lips. "I'll wait for you."

"And you still love me?"

"I never stopped, Lisa. I never stopped loving you. I've had other girlfriends, but no one compares to you. You're it for me. Say what you want, but I know what my heart wants." He brings my hand to his chest and holds it there. I feel his heart

Vision of Hope

beating and I close my eyes, taking in his words. Before I know it, our lips meet, and I don't let him go.

Ian spends more and more time at my apartment. I wake up and he's there. I go to bed and he's there. He knows about Jensen and doesn't push me to make a decision. I can't bring myself to talk to Jensen about this and ask for a break.

How can I love both men? Is that possible?

Walking around the village the next day, I sip on my latte from Starbucks and think about what I should tell Jensen. Does he even have to know? From what he's said before, his schedule is getting busier and he won't be able to see me as much. I've never been second in a man's life and I'm not going to start now. If Jensen can't be here for me, and Ian's willing, then I know what I'm doing and I'm not going to regret it. Sure, I'm being selfish, but I have needs and Ian's there to take care of my needs. I'm a very sexual person who needs to be properly fucked at least once a day.

Sexting isn't anything. It's boring. Child's play. Ian's my right now and Jensen's my future. I'm confident that this will work out and *if* Jensen finds out, he'll understand. We've been through several rough patches. This will be nothing for us to get over.

Sipping on my latte, I continue my walk, turning down to the canal. My phone vibrates in my pocket, alerting me of either a call or text message.

Jensen: *Hey, baby. We haven't talked in a while. What are you doing?*

Me: *Nothing really. Walking around the village, window shopping. It's a nice day out. I think I'm going to go for a run soon. Who knows?*

Jensen: *I miss you. Thinking about you a lot and hoping you're okay.*

Me: *Yeah. I'm fine =) Promise.*

Ian: *Hey, I just got to your place and you aren't here. Feeling dirty?*

Me: *Why? What do you have in mind?*

Jensen: *Well, I feel bad that I'm not there to make sure you're okay. But you should head back home soon.*

Me: *I'm walking to my car now.*

Ian: *Does that mean I get to see your sexy ass soon? Because I've been thinking about licking your ass and making you come. You want that, babe? You want my tongue inside you? You need my tongue, huh? Can't get enough because, fuck, just sitting here thinking about your sweet pussy and ass is getting me hard.*

Me: *I'll be home soon.*

Chapter 18
Jensen

It's five in the morning and I'm out running with Fallyn. It's five. In. The. Morning. I've been sleeping like shit, so it's not like it matters. Being out here so early isn't what I had in mind. I look over at Fallyn as she runs. So carefree, while I'm struggling to make it through the day. I hate being ignored by Lisa. Every day, it's something that she makes me feel shitty about. My job and responsibilities shouldn't get in the way of our relationship. I'm fucking working my ass off to give her a future so she doesn't have to worry. I don't want her worrying about anything else except graduating and then coming back home to me and her family.

"Doing okay?" I nod. "Seriously, Jensen, what's up with you?"

"Nothing," I breathe in through my nose and out through my mouth. "Just relationship problems. Everything I do, Lisa gets upset." I stop running and she follows suit. Taking out my phone, I open my text messages and hand my cell to Fallyn.

Lisa: *You're always working! I miss you and need you, Jensen.*

Me: *I'm trying my hardest to work here and come see you. I'm sorry that I haven't had the chance.*

Lisa: *I needed you a few weeks ago and you NEVER even came!*

Me: *What are you talking about? Wandering off? Do you want a break? What do you want?*

Lisa: *I want my BOYFRIEND to love me and want to spend time with me!*

Me: *Lisa, what the fuck do you think I'm doing? I work all the time! I hardly see anyone and I missed Emma's recital.*

Lisa: *I'm your girlfriend, though. The woman you love and want to spend your life with. Sometimes I wonder if we should take a break. You're always so busy, I might as well be single!*

Me: *I don't know what you want me to say. I love you and I know we'll be okay. I'm sorry that I'm making you feel this way.*

"That's it? She hasn't responded?"

"No." I walk away, continuing down the trail. "She's changing into someone I don't know. I have no idea what to do. I fucking love her, but if she can't see what I'm doing and how hard I'm working, then what's the point?"

Fallyn's hand rests on my shoulder. She comes around and faces me. "Because love conquers all. If you believe your love for Lisa is strong enough, then you'll be able to get through this. Love shouldn't be about all of this. She's stressed out and so are you. Don't talk to one another if you're feeling down or upset. Words are said and it's not fair to either of you. Take some time and maybe go see her. Like you said, she's never been in love before and you're her first serious boyfriend."

Her words register in my head. I'm looking at this all wrong. I remember what it was like to go through college and all of my courses. The endless amount of time spent studying and doing homework. I'm sure repeating most of her classes isn't easy on her either.

"I'm an asshole, huh?"

"Nope. Just human."

"All right, smart ass. Wanna finish this run?"

"Ready, set..." And she takes off laughing, leaving me behind.

I can't get what Fallyn said out of my head. I'm sitting in my office, looking at my emails, and everything blurs together. I think about texting Lisa and see how she's doing, but I stop myself. I don't know what she needs. Does she need space? I know she needs me and wants me there. Sometimes, I wish I could pick up and leave Wilmington, but Emma, my job, and friends mean a lot to me. Dread consumes me, leaving regret and guilt to fester and grow. How will I know what decision will be right?

I pick up my phone and call Lisa. I'm sure she's in class and won't answer. I need her to hear my voice. Her voicemail picks up and I take a deep breath before letting it out.

Beep.

"Hey, baby, it's me. I'm sorry about everything. I'm sorry that I haven't been making time for you. You're right. You're my girlfriend and the woman I want to spend the rest of my life with. I hope you realize and know how much you mean to me and how much I love you. Have a great day and call me later. I love you, baby."

I put my head down on the desk and close my eyes. She'll be back during breaks and summer. This is only temporary. There's a knock on my office door.

"Hey," I look up and see Karly with Sebastian in her arms. "Wanna grab lunch?" I nod my head and walk over to them. "God, you do look like s-h-i-t."

"Why are you spelling?"

Her eyes go to Sebastian, then back to me. "I don't want my son swearing!"

"He's not even one yet." I laugh, placing my hand on the small of her back and walking out of my office.

All throughout lunch, I've been thinking about Lisa and checking my phone. No text message or a phone call. Nothing.

"So I'm thinking about leaving Nicholas and running away to become a singer. What do you think?"

"Sounds great, sweetheart. You'll be fine."

"Do you think I should try out for *American Idol*?"

"Huh?" What the hell is she talking about? "I'm sorry. You lost me."

"What's going on with you?" Karly reaches across the table and places her hand on top of mine. I need this connection with her. There's nothing romantic between us. She's an important person to me.

"I wish I knew what was going on. It's just this whole thing with Lisa and we're on different pages. It's a f-u-c-k-e-d up situation."

Karly leans back in her chair and crosses her arms. "You knew how Lisa is, though. I'm not trying to say I told you so. Lisa's great and I love her, but she's also way younger than you. You're both on different levels and want different things. I know I'm a b-i-t-c-h for telling you this, but I wouldn't be your best friend if I didn't."

There's not much to say after that. We finish our lunch and she invites me over tomorrow night for dinner. Walking back to the hospital, I feel a heavy weight on my shoulders. Getting on the elevator, I look at my phone again.

Nothing.

Hating the idea of spending another night in a quiet house, I send a text to Fallyn, asking her if she wants to grab dinner.

Fallyn: *Sure thing. Wanna meet at my place?*

Me: *Sounds good. An hour good?*

Fallyn: *More like 10 min. LOL.*

Jaw to the floor. I've *never* known a woman who can get ready in minutes. Usually, I'm waiting way over an hour.

Me: *Okay, see you then.*

Chapter 19
Fallyn

I'm doing everything I can to make time go slowly. Tonight, Jensen and I are going out to dinner and I've been thinking about any excuse I can not to go. I can't believe I told him I'd be ready in ten minutes. Did that seem too desperate?

Pulling up my leggings and throwing on a gray tunic sweater, I walk back to the living room and look at Brody. Having his picture out here in the living room brings a peace that helps me relax. I like knowing he's in almost each room of my house, watching me, listening to me, and protecting me.

"I've been thinking about something lately. So I know you told me to move on and be happy, but did you mean it?" Silence. "It's hard for me to wrap my head around that. You're the only person I've been with and we shared all of our firsts together. It's hard for me to think about being with someone else. I know I'm young and I have my whole life, but that was reserved for you and me. I would never replace you. You'll always be in my heart. I'm so confused, Brody." Silence.

I look up and stare at our pictures. He's so handsome, standing there with his arms around me and the biggest smile on his face. "You always made me smile whenever I was down." I sigh, twirling my blonde hair between my fingers. "So I'm going out tonight with Jensen. He's nice and I'm glad he's my friend, but is it okay?" No answer. I know he'll never answer me, but it brings me comfort knowing I can talk to him and, in my heart, I know he's listening. "Like I said, he's a friend. I like being around him. Just feel bad, ya know?" I take a seat on my couch and pull my knees up to my chest. "His girlfriend, Lisa, well, she seems kinda bitchy. You should have read the messages. I think you would have rolled your eyes and told him to get rid of her. I kinda wanted to, but it's not my place. Brody, do you think I should tell him to grow balls?" No answer again. I lean back and think about my own question. Jensen's a great guy, and Lisa seems like a bitch. Even though we've never met, and I know I'm passing judgment too quickly. I'm pretty good with reading people and seeing past their bullshit. I can definitely smell bullshit. Pulling out my phone, I send a text to Isaac.

Me: *Need advice.*

Isaac: *Shoot.*

Me: *I have a friend who is awesome, but his girlfriend is a bitch! What should I do?*

Isaac: *Be there for him when he needs you and support his relationship. Can't interfere with love, sis.*

Me: *You're right.*

Isaac: *Now I need your advice.*

Me: *Shoot!*

Isaac: *So my friend Ian is in love with his ex. I guess they've been hanging out and doing things that they shouldn't be doing. Sis, she has a boyfriend and she's fucking Ian on the side. He's sure she's using him. Hell, even I know that. Wtf do I do?*

Me: *Be there for him when he needs you and support his relationship. Can't interfere with love, sweetie.*

Isaac: *You can't give me my own advice! Fine, whatever. I'll shut up. But I feel bad for whoever her boyfriend is. She's demanding and rude. I'm going up in a few days, so I'll be sure to give you the play by play.*

Me: *Please do. I love drama. Haha jk. K, gotta run! Talk soon. Love ya!*

Isaac: *Love ya more, sis.*

Vision of Hope

As I read Isaac's last text message, my doorbell rings. I get up from the couch and skip over to the door.

"Helllllo." I smile with my singsong voice, opening the door and leaning against the frame. I take in what he's wearing – dark fitted jeans and a blue button-down. My eyes go wide. Jaw meet floor. Oh, sweet baby Jesus. *Calm yourself, Fallyn. Down, girl!*

"Hey! You ready?"

"Sure am!" I grab my clutch and meet Jensen on the porch. Getting a closer look at him, I rake his body with my wide eyes and devour each muscle line. As if he can feel me staring, he turns around and gives me a panty-dropping smile.

Fallyn! You are not a home wrecker. Stop staring at your FRIEND. Who cares if he's incredibly sexy and his muscles are delicious enough to lick. Who cares if his eyes remind you of the ocean, so calm and peaceful. And who cares if his smile is making you melt to the ground and your heart beating against your chest. He's your FRIEND. F-R-I-E-N-D!

"Ready to go?"

"Yep!" I hop down from the step and walk a little in front of him, needing some space to breathe so I'm not drooling all over him. He catches up to me and walks a little too close. My body registers how close he is and blows an alarm. *Warning! Warning! Man next to you smells amazing!* Oh, I'm so dead.

Jensen opens the passenger door for me and I comfortably get in, sitting on my hands to stop them from shaking. This is so bad. We've been out before and we work together, so why am I acting like this?

Needing to take my mind off him, I look at the interior of his Mustang. "I would love to drive your car one day!"

"She's my baby. *No one* has driven her before."

"You don't trust me?" I bat my lashes to him. I shoot him a mocking smile and turn in my seat to talk to him. "But we're pretty good friends."

"You know how adorable you are when you try to negotiate?" He's grinning, and I notice the grip around the steering wheel gets a bit tighter. "But no. I'm the only one who gets to drive my car."

"Oh come on," I say playfully. "This car is beautiful. Seriously, I could totally get off while driving her." My hands go to my mouth and I turn back in my seat. *Stupid! Stupid! Stupid!* I cannot believe I said that. Maybe he didn't hear me. Peeking from the corner of my eye, I see there's a wide grin on his face and he's shaking his head.

I just want to die.

Chapter 20
Jensen

We get to a little Italian restaurant and are immediately seated in a booth. The dark corner is quiet and the atmosphere is nice. There are a few other tables around us. Since living here, I've never noticed this place.

"Do you come here often?"

"Oh yeah. I love this place. Me and Italian food are like this." She lifts her hand and crosses her index and middle fingers. "Brody got me to love Italian." She laughs, but quietly frowns and looks down. The smile on her face is gone and my heart beats wildly against my chest.

"Fallyn. You okay?"

Her eyes catch mine, gazing at me as she searches for an answer. I'm not sure what exactly she's looking for while looking at me. My smile grows, hoping to ease her tension and have her open up.

"No matter how much time passes, I'm always going to miss him. It's getting easier and I'm not sure why. It's like there's a weight lifted off my shoulders and, for the first time, I can breathe. I like knowing that I'm looking forward to tomorrow. I was a mess when Brody died. I didn't want to be around anyone." She pauses and takes a few deep breaths. "I think I have you to thank for my mood."

"Me?"

She nods. "Yeah, you. You've been a great friend and I love hanging out with you." Our hands rest within one another and we sit in silence. She's right. For the first time in a while, I feel different. I can't explain it as elegantly as she did, but it's something I understand and feel. I'm not sure what to think anymore.

"Any more luck with Lisa?"

"Same old."

"If I can be honest."

"Sure."

"You seem so unhappy. I don't like seeing you so upset. Is there anything I can do to help you?"

"You are." Her smile triggers my own smile and soon I find that our conversation is flowing nicely and we're talking about random things.

And I like it.

* * * * *

I wake up the next morning to several angry messages from Lisa.

Why aren't you answering my phone calls?

Jensen! How can you already be sleeping?

What are you doing?

Seriously, I need to talk to you!

Giving her a call, it goes straight to voicemail. I call her a few more times and get the same thing. Deciding to leave her a message, I apologize to her for missing her phone calls and hope that she's okay. I tell her to call me back as soon as she can.

How can we go from doing okay to this? The roller coaster of our relationship is coming to a stop and it's going to happen now. There's only so much I can take from her.

Getting ready for the day, I leave my house and check my phone. Still nothing from Lisa. I try calling her again and get her voicemail. "Fuck," I mumble.

Pulling into my parking spot, I call her again and leave her another message, asking her why her phone is off and to call my office phone. These are childish games and I know she's

Vision of Hope

doing this on purpose. She's done it before and I'm not surprised she's doing it again.

My office door opens and Fallyn comes in. "Morning."

"Hey, Fallyn. What's going on?"

"Nothing. Just wanted to pop in and say hi and let you know that you're wearing the same tie…Again."

I look down at my blue tie, rubbing my eyes together. So I've been a mess these past few days. Everything was great until Lisa had one of her moments and screamed at me. I don't get her hot and cold attitude. . I know it's been a while since we've seen each other and I know she needs me. I can't stop what I'm doing to rush over to her. The trip isn't short and it's not like I can get in my car and be there in a few minutes. The way things are going with the hospital, I most likely won't see her until she's home for Thanksgiving. My mind is everywhere. "Things with Lisa are weird again." I stop typing an email and turn to face her. "I have no idea what I'm doing wrong. I sent her flowers and a card with a teddy bear and nothing. It's like she and I don't exist. One day we'll be great and the next she turns into someone I don't fucking know. I can't keep up. What am I supposed to do?"

"Why don't you go visit her?"

"Did you hear what I said? The way the hospital is going, it's not easy for me to pick up and leave. I've been swamped here at the hospital. Every time I think I'm going to have some time off, something comes up. She says she understands, but I know she's upset. We're both busy, and I'm trying to get her to understand why I can't leave my position here at the hospital." I get up from my desk and pace my office. "I've worked so hard getting to this position. I'm the youngest medical director and look what I've done. Why can't she see that?"

I don't want to be that boyfriend who hounds his girlfriend and needs her attention all the time, but some would be nice.

"Go."

"What?"

She smiles. "Go! Here's a plane ticket to Rochester. Bethany is going to take care of your meetings and emails today. This is why you have an assistant director. You need to put Lisa first and just go! It leaves in a few hours." She hands me the tickets and pulls me away from my desk. I'm thoroughly confused.

Shocked isn't the word I'm looking for. "What?"

"You're not yourself and you need to get away this weekend. A few of the nurses and I got this for you. Plus, you've been in the *worst* mood ever. We're scared for our lives!"

So I admit I haven't been nice to be around and I've been yelling more. "Scared for your lives?" She nods. I get up and give Fallyn a hug. "Thank you."

In a few hours, I'll be with Lisa and, hopefully, when I come back, things will be back to normal.

* * * * *

Nervously standing at Lisa's door, I use my key and walk in. It's quiet inside. I know she should be home from clinical. I check the time and see it's almost six in the evening. Maybe she's out with her friends for dinner. Placing my bags down, I look around her apartment and notice a few things out of place. Our pictures aren't in the living room. I walk into the kitchen and see pictures of us in groups, but never side by side. Ignoring my thoughts, I grab a vase from one of the cabinets and place it on the island with her favorite pink roses.

On our first date, I brought her red roses and she quickly grabbed them from my hand and threw them in the trash. I stood there confused, but smiled.

"Rule one when dating me. Roses only can be pink. No red, yellow, white, orange. Just pink."

I take her hand in mine, leaning down to kiss her cheek. "Okay. Only pink."

Heading down the hall to Lisa's room, I hear soft noises coming from her room.

"Ahhh... harder. Ian! Oh, shit! Oh, shit!"

My heart falls and stops beating. Everything around me goes blank. I stand a few feet from her door, listening to her moans. I can't move or turn away. Lisa. The girl I love and want to spend my life with is cheating on me with someone else.

Her nails are digging in his back, with her legs wrapped around his waist. His thrusts grow faster and suddenly slow. Our eyes meet.

"Jensen! Jensen!" Pushing Ian off her, she runs to me, straightening her dress and looking at me. "I can explain." I don't say anything. I glance at Ian and he's putting on his clothes, staying the hell away from me. Her hands touch my face, turning it to face her. "Look at me," she cries. "I'm sorry. I'm so sorry. The distance and stress got to me. I'm so confused, Jensen. So lost and scared. I love the both of you, but I need you to understand. I love you, Jensen."

I place my hands on top of hers, kiss her forehead, and walk out into the kitchen. There are no words needed for how I'm feeling. I can yell at her, make her cry, and beat the shit out of Ian. But what will that do for me? It won't change how I feel. It won't bring her back.

I grab my bag, reach inside, and place the small box on the island next to her pink roses.

Chapter 21
Fallyn

Things have been steady lately. I don't like steady. Steady means things are going on behind the scenes and change is going to happen soon.

For instance, Jensen's taking some time off and I'm not sure what's going on with him. He's not responding to my messages or calls and it's not like I can go over to his house and check on him. But the boundaries stopping me force me to take a step back. I remind myself he has a girlfriend and I shouldn't have feelings for him. But it's been a week since I last saw him. Something's wrong.

"Have you talked to him?" Lexi asks me and Karly. Both of us shake our heads no.

"He came to see Emma and spent time with her two days ago, but he didn't wanna talk. Have you talked to Lisa?"

Lexi shakes her head, playing with her food. "Nope. I tried texting her and she hasn't texted me back. Do you think they're fighting?"

"No idea. Lemme text him," Karly says, putting down her napkin and pulling out her phone.

I pull out my phone and text Jensen too, hoping he'll talk to me. This is the longest we've gone without talking and I'm worried about him. I have a bad feeling the trip to see Lisa didn't end well.

Me: *Hey, what's going on? Where are you? I'm worried about you. We haven't talked in a while.*

Vision of Hope

Jensen: *Sorry about that. I didn't mean to make you think I was ignoring you, but I'm fine. Going through a lot right now.*

Me: *Anything I can do?*

Jensen: *Can you turn back time?*

Me: *Nope. Sorry. I can bring smiles and hugs, though.*

Jensen: *Thanks. Not what I'm looking for.*

Karly pouts. "So Stephen said that Jensen's isn't really talking to him. When I asked about Lisa, he ignored my question, so I think something bad happened."

"It's so weird," Lexi adds. "Let me text Lisa again."

So this goes on for a while. Karly talking to Stephen and Lexi talking to Lisa.

Me: *Are you and Lisa okay?*

Jensen: *Why?*

Oh boy.

Me: *Jensen...I'm here if you need to talk.*

Jensen: *I caught her fucking some dude. The ticket you got me, yep, surprise. I was gonna propose to her, ya know? Make it official. I would have done anything for her. Moved mountains, crossed oceans...Anything.*

Me: *I'm really sorry. Have you tried talking to her?*

Jensen: *No.*

Me: *I'm not that experienced in the relationship field, but if you caught her cheating on you...You deserve to know why and what she was thinking. I feel awful this happened. I'm sorry we got you the ticket and made you go.*

Jensen: *You have nothing to be sorry about. I don't blame you and it's not even crossed my mind. I should thank you, actually. Things with Lisa started to get rocky and now I understand why.*

I read his message a few times. I know it's not my fault, but part of me feels like it is. I'm the one who came up with the idea to get him a ticket so he could go see her. If that didn't happen, he wouldn't have caught her. But then again, I'm glad he did. I've never been cheated on, so I have no idea how that would feel. But I'm sure it's the one of the worst feelings—*betrayal.*

Me: *I'm sorry, and if you need anything, please let me know. Okay?*

Jensen: *Oh, I'm fine. I'm remodeling my house right now.*

Oh boy.

Me: *Do you want me to stop by later?*

Jensen: *Sure. Bring Jack. I'm almost out.*

"So Jensen and Lisa broke up," I whisper.

"WHAT!" they both screech.

"Ow." I rub my ears. "Yeah, Jensen said he found her and some guy having sex."

"Whoa, what!" Karly yells, pushing out the chair, pressing a few buttons on her phone, and bringing it to her ear. "Are you kidding me right now?" She pauses. "Are you okay?" She pauses again. "We'll be right there." When she hangs up, she motions for us to get up and we head out the door. Tonight's going to be interesting.

When we get to Jensen's house, things are a little crazy. There's loud noise coming from the living room and lots of weird grunting noises.

"Jensen, dude, I'm sorry!" We run to the living room and find Stephen on the floor. Lexi and Karly go to Stephen, helping him sit up, and I stand next to Jensen, holding him back.

"You fucking knew she was cheating on me!" he screams, "You fucking knew!" His voice croaks, "You knew."

Stephen struggles to get up and wipes the blood from his nose. "I'm sorry. I didn't know what else to do. It's shady of me to have kept it from you and, yeah, you're my friend, but that's my baby sister, man."

Jensen turns around and walks away. He pulls the framed pictures from his walls, smashing each one on the floor. I reach out to touch his shoulder and feel his body stiffen and tense.

"Jensen," Karly slowly says, "please stop what you're doing and talk to us."

"What's there to say?" he mutters. "The girl I was going to ask to marry cheated on me and all she can say is 'sorry.' I'm fucking sick of hearing 'sorry.' I'm fucking sick of being treated like a fucking nobody."

"Don't think that way," I chime in.

"Really?" He turns around and faces us. His eyes are bloodshot red and his face is so pale. "Let's review my life. Jamie screwed me over and took away *my* daughter. Now I have to spend the rest of my life being called 'Uncle Jensen' and she'll only know me as that. My best friend and her husband are going to raise her and experience moments that I'll never get to. Lisa has been fucking some guy and didn't have the fucking balls to tell me." I look over and see Karly's head go down and, instantly, my heart breaks. She wipes tears from her eyes. Lexi places her arm around her shoulders and gives Jensen a menacing look.

"You can't control what Jamie did. They've apologized to you, but don't act like the victim, Jensen!" Lexi screams. "You fooled all of us and knew what Jamie was doing. All three of you agreed that keeping this from Emma was the best thing to do."

"I know! I fucking remember!"

"Calm down, man." Stephen pushes him to the corner of the room. "Just calm down." Jensen rubs his face, pushing his hands into his hair and turning around, punching the wall.

"Ugh!" He punches the wall a few more times before falling to the ground. "I was going to fucking ask her to marry me," is all he says before closing his eyes and letting his hands fall to the ground.

"Lexi, take the girls home," Stephen says, picking Jensen up and bringing him to the couch.

"Are you sure?" He nods. "Okay. Come on, girls."

"I'm gonna stay if that's all right." Everyone looks at me, but no one says anything. Lexi and Karly give me a hug before leaving. Standing in the living room with Stephen and Jensen makes me suddenly feel uneasy. I'm not sure how to help him overcome this hurdle.

Leaving the room, I walk into the kitchen and start cleaning. Stephen isn't saying anything, and neither am I. About an hour passes before the kitchen and living room are clean. We head outside on his deck and sit down, neither of us still saying anything.

"I thought it would be a onetime thing with Ian and she'd tell him." He shakes his head. "Fuck, I feel like an asshole."

"Ian?"

"Yeah," he slowly says.

"Oh, shit. If this is the same Ian, then Isaac asked me advice about this, saying how he's in love with her and wants to be with her." I quickly get out my phone and ask Isaac about Ian.

Isaac: *Yeah! The girl's name is Lisa!*

Me: *You idiot! Jensen and Lisa!*

Isaac: *Oh damn, small world. Well, I guess you don't want to know that he's with her now.*

Me: *No, I didn't want to know =(*

"Ian's with Lisa now."

"Oh, shit." Stephen leans in, shaking his head. "What a fucking mess."

"So Lisa's with Ian now? The guy she fucking screwed me over with," Jensen roars, picking up the bottle of Jack and throwing it against the wall. "Everything! I would have given you fucking everything."

Vision of Hope

    Stephen and I run to Jensen. I throw my arms around his middle and hold him tight. He fights me and yells at us to let him go. Before I know it, we're on his living room floor and he's not fighting us anymore.

Chapter 22
Jensen

Every time I wake up, the days and nights merge together. I reach for the bottle each time I wake up, drinking to numb myself, to make myself forget. I'm falling and I can't stop falling. I don't look down because I'm afraid to see the truth—no one would be there at the bottom with me.

Blackness surrounds me, fogging my thoughts and making it hard to think. But I like that because if I don't think, then I can't feel, and I can't feel the empty space where Lisa used to be. To help not feel, I drink and when I drink to the point of blacking out, I can sleep and forget about the shit around my life.

Sometimes, when I close my eyes, I see her being fucked by Ian. I hear her moans in my head and all I want is to punch the shit out of him and shake her into explaining why. Cheating is the one unforgivable thing. Once the trust is gone, it's hard to get it back. Part of me hates her, but the other part loves her.

I ask myself what I did wrong. *Did I push her away? Did I give her enough?*

All of these questions plague my mind. But at the end of the day, I realize this isn't my fault. I did everything for her and loved her with everything that I am. Because when you love someone, you love them. You show them your love with your words and actions. You cherish them and make each moment count.

Vision of Hope

But here I am. A man standing in the middle of the room, naked and scared, because the direction in his life is unclear.

There's a knock on my door, but I don't get up from the couch to get it. "Jensen?" Her voice rings in the house.

Fallyn.

When she walks into the room, she stands in front of me, holding two bags. I wonder why she's here. For the past few days, she and Stephen have been permanent visitors, even though I don't want them here. I don't want anyone here.

"Get ready."

"For what?"

"We're going to spend the day at Greenfield Lake Park! Five miles of hiking and you need it. We haven't been running and you need to get your mind off everything."

I scoff, not looking at her. "Go home, Fallyn. I'm not in the mood for you today."

She walks in front of me, putting down the bags. Her hands are on her thighs and her eyes meet mine. When I try to look away, she takes my face so that we're facing each other once again. "I am not taking no for an answer. You need to get up and get out of this house. You need to spend some time outside, letting go of everything in your mind, then go and apologize to your friends who love you and don't want to see you like this."

Quickly, I get up and pace the room. "My life has been a fucking mess!"

"So? Do something about it, Jensen! You caught her cheating and it sucks, but your life isn't over! You're still here! Your friends are still here! Stop moping around and man up!"

"Man up?" I laugh, instantly wanting to punch something or someone. "You have *no* idea what the fuck I'm going through."

"Oh really?" She laughs, sitting down on the couch, turning to face me. "The night of my high school graduation, my parents and sister, Nicole, were driving to the ceremony to watch me walk the stage and get my diploma. They were only five miles away when someone crashed into their car. The driver of the other car was on her cell phone and wasn't paying attention. She walked away, but my family died. Brody died in my arms because of his crazy ex-girlfriend. I tried committing suicide. Did you know that? Yeah, when Brody died, I thought about taking pills so I wouldn't have to live my life without him. But something happened and I realized I need to live for myself and for Brody. So yeah, Jensen, I know what the fuck pain is. I know what it's like to wake up and not get out of bed. But you move on and live your life. You can't sit in the shadows and watch life pass you by. I promised myself that I was going to live, and little by little, I *am* living. You need to make that promise to yourself, so get ready and let's go!"

I'm not sure what to say. This woman sitting in front of me bared her soul and let me in. She's been through pain and saw death before her eyes while I'm standing before her, nursing a broken heart. Fuck, I feel like a pussy.

Nodding my head, I walk upstairs and change into workout clothes. In about ten minutes, we're out the door. The drive to the park isn't long. We're quiet in the car, but out of the corner of my eye, I see her smile. For some reason, I like seeing her smile. I like sitting in the car with Fallyn and feeling like I can breathe.

I can breathe.

Placing my hand on her thigh, I give it a squeeze, but neither of us says anything. She places her hand on top of mine and lets out a small sigh.

As soon as I find a parking spot, I run to Fallyn's side and open the door for her. "Thanks, handsome." She smiles. "Ready?" I nod. Still not sure how to feel or what to say. It's been a while since I've been out of the house. It feels strange, but the good kind of strange, if that makes sense. Fallyn's small hand takes mine and, even though she doesn't think this gesture means anything, to me, it means everything. I feel good around her and I don't have to hide how I feel. She understands pain and has embraced it. Am I embracing my pain?

The way her hand fits in mine doesn't go unnoticed. My chest rises and falls and, in the pit of my stomach, I feel something. It's hard to explain, but in many ways, it isn't. The thought of spending days upon days locked in my house sickens me. I didn't do anything wrong and I need to move on with my life. To me, I can give myself time to heal and get over her, but the sight of her being fucked by some other guy is more than enough for me to realize our love wasn't strong enough.

We head to the trails and walk. Being outside, surrounded by the natural beauty of nature, is peaceful. The weight on my shoulders and my heart slowly dissipates. Breathing in and out, I realize that I never took the time to take in the beauty around me. The tall trees and birds chirping set my mind at ease.

The silence between Fallyn and me grows. I want to say something, but it's too peaceful and I don't want to taint this memory with thoughts of Lisa. Since coming back home, after catching Lisa with someone else, things are dark and blurry. After dealing with one thing after another with Jamie, I thought that meeting Lisa was my saving grace. I thought she was the one to make everything better, but I was wrong. I was wrong again.

I hate the fucking pity party I'm throwing myself. I'm the only one attending and everyone's declined. No one wants to hear the shit going on in my head. *I* don't want to hear the shit going through my head. Clenching my fists, I close my eyes and steady my breathing. The rage inside me grows and I want to punch something.

Her hand touches my arm and, instantly, I unclench my fists and my heart races. My breathing quickens. I open my eyes and there she is. She's standing in front of me and behind her is the sun, the rays shining down around her. She looks like an angel. A beautiful angel. My beautiful friend who hasn't left my side.

I bring her in my arms, holding her close. Her arms wrap around my waist. I kiss the top of her head, close my eyes, and slowly breathe. Everything around me is peaceful. The rage disappears and, in this moment, it's just me and Fallyn.

Just me and Fallyn.

I realize that I'm falling for her. The feelings are wide open and I'm sinking into her touch. Reality creeps in my head. It hasn't been a month and I'm already falling for another woman. Then again, I wonder if these feelings have been inside me for a while and now coming to my head because it's okay.

"Fallyn?"

"Yes?"

"Thank you for this." Our eyes meet and I look at her soft lips. Licking my own, I lean forward and lightly brush my lips to hers.

"Jensen," she utters softly.

"Thank you." I kiss her again.

* * * * *

I sit at my table, listening to Isaac and Stephen talk. It's been a few days since the hike with Fallyn and she's all I can think about.

"Man, I'm sorry again I didn't tell you. I didn't connect Ian and Lisa," Isaac explains.

I take a swig of my beer. "No worries, man. You didn't know."

Vision of Hope

"I did, though," Stephen adds and drinks his beer. "You gotta understand, man. She's my sister."

"I get it. It's no one's fault except Lisa's. She put everyone in a bad position and now she has to live with the consequences of her actions. I'm not going back to her."

My mind reels back to the kiss at the park with Fallyn. I'm not surprised I'm falling for her. What's there not to fall for? She's beyond gorgeous with a big heart. She's smart, funny, knows how to live, and she's not allowing her past to keep her down. I smile, thinking about her and the look on her face when I kissed her. She's been waiting for my kiss and I want more.

"Jensen! Dude? You dreaming?"

I lean forward, not being able to stop thinking about her.

"I think he's thinking about a girl," Isaac says to Stephen.

"But who?"

"Ladies, wanna get going or do you two need a few more minutes to gossip about my life?"

The both of them look at me and cock their heads to the side at the same time. I can't help but laugh at how idiotic they look.

"Okay, let's go."

Stephen pulls me aside. "It's okay that you want to move on. You don't have to explain yourself to anyone. What Lisa did to you is fucked up and if you want to move on now, then do it. Don't let your life slide away because you're pining over a girl."

"I'm falling for Fallyn." Saying it aloud and feeling the way my body reacts to saying her name makes me feel better. I know I have to give myself time to get over Lisa, which isn't hard to do. I don't want to be a dick, especially since her brother is my best friend, but she's dead to me. I don't deserve to be treated the way she's been treating me.

"That's great, man. She's one of the good ones and I hope she feels the same about you. Keep an open mind with her and remember that the both of you deserve love." He pauses. "I take that back. I know she feels that way about you, but don't push her."

"I know. I won't." All I can see is her beautiful blue eyes and long, blonde hair. She's looking at me and waiting for me to come to her. The thought of being with her, holding her in my arms, is all I need to make sure she'll be mine soon.

Chapter 23
Lisa

I've been at the airport for the past hour. I'm not sure what I'm doing back in Wilmington. Things have been so hard since Jensen walked out of my apartment. Ian's been giving me space so I can think. All I can think about is the ring he left behind. I ruined it all. The look on his face is deep in my head. I can't stop thinking about him and what I did. I've been thinking about ways to get him back, to make him understand and forgive me. Letting Jensen go, watching him walk away from me, was the biggest mistake of my life. Being with Ian was a mistake too. I should have stopped it with him, but part of me couldn't. Part of me wants to be with Ian. Ian's more like me—we're both fun and young. Jensen's great, and he'll take care of me.

Both guys are incredible.

But there's only one who I want and need.

Jensen.

Finally getting the courage I need, I get in my rental, start the car, and head to Jensen's house. The easy drive is the hardest I've had to take. I keep my eyes focused, but my palms are sweaty and I want to throw up. My head is spinning. I open the windows and feel the cool breeze flowing through the car. Breathing in and out, I step a little harder on the gas and gun it to his house.

Taking the final left turn, I slow down and pass three houses until I come to his. But what I see is not what I'm expecting.

Rushing out of the car, I walk up the driveway and through the front door. Making my way to the kitchen, I stop and see someone putting things away.

"Fallyn?" She turns around and I nearly die from laughing. Is this real life? Did Jensen seriously replace me with Shamu? "Ummm, hi, why are you in Jensen's house? I know you're not his girlfriend. Jensen doesn't date..." I wave my hand up and down her body, "...bigger girls."

"Lisa." I turn around and see Jensen standing in the entryway. "What the fuck are you doing here?"

"Baby." I walk over to him, placing my hand on his arm, but he pulls away. "Baby, I wanted to talk. I think we've been apart for too long and now, since we're both calm, we can talk."

"No."

"Excuse me?"

"No," he says again. "There's nothing to talk about, Lisa. You did what you did and I've moved on."

"Jensen, you don't just let go of a yearlong relationship. We're in love and we can work this out. We can get through this."

He shakes his head, looking at Shamu, then back at me. "You need to apologize to Fallyn."

"Why?"

Before he can respond, she starts talking. "I don't appreciate you coming into my friend's house and yelling at me. I like how I look and I'm not fat. It's called curves! I'm healthy and fit and have muscle, unlike you. You look like you need about ten cheeseburgers and a side of fries."

"No, sweetie, that's something you eat. I take care of myself."

"I take care of myself too. Sorry I'm not a size zero like you. Well, actually, I'm not sorry. I love my body and I've never heard any complaints."

"Maybe not to your face."

"Lisa, leave. Just get out." Jensen stands next to Fallyn, putting his arm around her shoulders. "If you cannot apologize to her, then you need to leave. There's nothing for us to talk about. You did what you did and I'm moving on. I deserve better. I deserve a woman who will stay faithful and appreciate me."

"I do!" I stomp, staring at him. "I made a mistake, Jensen. I'm so sorry that I did that to you. Please, we can work this out."

"No, please leave. There's nothing for us to talk about."

Fallyn smirks at me and I almost lose it. Jensen notices my clenched fists and lets go of Fallyn. He walks over to me and places his hands on my shoulders, turning me around. "Leave, Lisa. I don't want to call Stephen to come get you."

"Fine." I don't turn around and look at him. "But this isn't over." I storm out of his house and head to Karly's. I need my best friends.

Running inside Karly's house and into her kitchen, I see Lexi, Larry, and Nicholas standing around.

"I really need you girls," I cry, sitting down at the island and taking Nicholas' beer.

"Lisa?" Lexi says, taking back the beer. "Okay, first, *HI,* and what the hell are you doing here? When did you get here?"

"Today. Just now. I went to Jensen's and met his fat girlfriend or whatever."

Nicholas and Larry look at each other and leave the kitchen. Neither Karly nor Lexi say anything and it's beginning to irritate me. I'm sitting here hurting and need my best friends. Why are they looking at me like I'm bothering them?

"Okay, can either of you say anything? I'm freaking a mess here."

"Lisa," Karly starts to say. "First, don't talk shit about Fallyn. She didn't do anything wrong and she's been there for Jensen after he found you cheating on him! I mean, my God, what the fuck were you thinking?"

"I wasn't okay!" I shout. "I mean, my fucking boyfriend never came to see me and I got lonely. It was really hard and I messed up."

"And did you learn?" Lexi asks.

I shrug. "Ian and I haven't talked. He's fun and I like him, but I love Jensen and know he can provide for me. He'll take care of me like he promised."

"I don't even know what to say." Karly throws her hands in the air. "Do you hear yourself? Do you even feel bad at all?"

"What are you talking about?"

"You're pissed because Jensen has a *friend* and you're sitting here with no emotions. You're not crying or anything. I mean, I don't know; you just seem like whatever. Do you even care you hurt him?"

"First," I get up, pushing the chair in, "I do care and I'm not you!" I shout again.

"What the hell are you talking about?"

"You're the one who won't tell Emma the truth! You're having her think that Jensen's her uncle when he's her dad! You don't give a fucking shit about his feelings, so don't stand here and preach, bitch."

"Get out, Lisa," Nicholas says, coming around and pulling Karly to his side. Larry does the same to Lexi and all four of them look at me. "You're out of line and have no idea what you're talking about. Don't come into our home, disrespecting my wife and our friends and family."

"Hello! I'm your friend too! Did you all lose your fucking minds?"

"Leave, Lisa. Leave now. You are not welcome back into our home."

Vision of Hope

I look to Lexi for help, but she doesn't say anything. No one says anything. I pick up my purse and leave the house. There's nothing left for me in Wilmington. I've lost my friends, boyfriend, and I have no one. Stephen won't talk to me either and, since he's out of town, I can't go to him. So who do I have?

Chapter 24
Fallyn

I've been waking up at four in the morning every day so I can get to the gym and work out for a few hours before I go to work. The things Lisa said cut deep. I know I've never been skinny, but I know I'm not fat. I have curves, big boobs, and a big ass. I think I'm beautiful—a real woman—but her words are making me think otherwise.

Pushing myself on the treadmill, I reach the four-mile mark, get off, and go straight to the weights. I push my body to the limit and focus on my stomach and thighs. My muscles are aching. I've been working out twice a day and this is day five.

Placing the bar under my shoulders, I lift, squat, and lift myself back up. I focus on my breathing and look straight ahead. There's a mirror in front of me, capturing all of my imperfections. My rolls have rolls.

I push harder and continue squatting until I can't feel my legs. From squats, I complete core workouts and battle the voices in my head. I replace the venomous voices with mine. I'm screaming at myself to keep going and not give up.

Move it, fat ass.

Push harder!

Don't you want to be skinny?

Completing my routine, I grab my water bottle and head to the locker room. Opening my locker, I take out my supplements and take two capsules with large gulps of water.

Vision of Hope

Resting my head on the locker, I close my eyes and imagine myself with a tiny body with smaller boobs and a smaller ass.

Turning around, I look at myself in the mirror, lifting up my shirt, and instantly hating how I look. "I *am* fat," I whisper, touching my stomach and pinching the fat. "She's right. I'm fat. I'm not healthy." Tears fall from my eyes and I look away. I can't stand here and look at myself.

Heading to work, I walk inside and go straight to the nurses' station, check my patients' files, and start working.

"Morning." I turn and see Sheila sitting down next to me. "Oh my gosh, you have to try these muffins. So freaking good. It's like heaven in your mouth."

"No thank you," I mutter, keeping focus on the files.

"Oh, come on, Fallyn! It's so good. Just a taste."

Not wanting to get irritated and blow up on Sheila, I get up and smile. "No thank you. I'm going to check on Joey. I'll see you later."

* * * * *

I work through my lunch and take two more capsules. The pills are working and I haven't felt hungry or had any cravings. My energy is through the roof and I feel really good. Making my final rounds, I get my things, say bye to the other nurses, and head to the gym for my second session.

I haven't talked to Jensen today. He's been in meetings all day and said he'll talk to me tonight. I'm not sure if I want to talk to him or see him. If Lisa thinks I'm fat, then I don't want to know what Jensen thinks about me.

Before I'm able to get to my car, I hear my name being called. *Oh no.* Pretending like I don't hear him, I walk a little faster and press my car alarm to unlock my car.

"Fallyn! Wait up!" Turning around, I know it's too late. "Hey!"

"Hi." I smile.

"Why have you been avoiding me? Didn't you get my text about meeting for lunch today?"

"You had meetings and I was busy." I look everywhere but at him.

"Okay, that's understandable. What's wrong, though? Are you okay?"

"Yep. Fine. I need to head to the gym, so I'll talk to you later, okay?"

He eyes me for a few moments and then nods his head. "Sounds good." Leaning over, he gives me a quick hug and walks away. I'm panting. His smell hits my nose and I want to melt. I want to turn around and call out for him. I want him to come to the gym with me so he can see how hard I'm working to lose weight so maybe I'll look and feel better.

No one likes fat girls. And I'm a fat girl.

After a grueling few hours at the gym, I'm finally home, showered, and comfortable in bed. Lying down with my Kindle, I finish reading and start a new book. Reading takes me away to a new place. A place where I can swoon and smile because of the hot and sexy book boyfriends I meet.

As I finish chapter one of *Redemption* by Rebecca Brooke, my phone vibrates and I debate if I should answer it. Ignoring my phone, I start chapter two, but then my phone vibrates again. My curiosity gets the best of me and I look at my phone and see a few text messages.

Karly: *Hey, girl! Drinks tomorrow night?*

Lexi: *Come out with us tomorrow night!*

Jensen: *Hey, just wanted to see what you're doing. Wanna take a walk on the beach?*

I text Karly and Lexi and tell them I'll let them know about tomorrow night in the morning. I look at Jensen's text and wonder what I should say.

Me: *Not tonight. I'm so tired from working out...Double sessions =(*

Jensen: *Why are you working out so much?*

Is he serious?

Me: *Because I don't like the way I look...I'm fat and it sucks.*

Jensen: *Stop. Do NOT take what Lisa said to you seriously. She was pissed and took it out on you. You are NOT fat, Fallyn. You're absolutely beautiful and your sexy curves can make a man fall to his knees. I've seen how active you are and think you're incredibly sexy. You're not too girly at the gym and you push yourself. I admire a woman who takes care of her body and you do.*

Tears fall from my eyes. I hate crying about this. I need to be strong. Crying is for the weak. Crying means you've given up and I'm not giving up.

Me: *I appreciate you saying this to me, but you've never seen me naked. I hate how I look and I don't care about Lisa. I want to be skinny and I'll do what it takes, so don't sit there and tell me you think I'm beautiful and sexy because I'm not.*

He doesn't respond as quickly as before. I wait a few more minutes and put my phone on silent. Turning back to my book, I find I'm totally into Josh and his story, falling in love with his words, and completely swooning.

Then there's a knock on the door.

Groaning, I put down my Kindle and head to see who is at the door. Without looking through the peephole, I open the door and see Jensen standing in front of me. He's wearing sweat pants and a black t-shirt. A t-shirt that hugs his body and shows his sexy muscles. Oh God, the images I have of him.

Realizing that I'm only wearing a tank top and booty shorts, I quickly turn away and walk to my room. He grabs my arm and spins me around. "Don't."

"What are you doing here?"

"Don't run from me, Fallyn. I know that you have these ideas about yourself and you're wrong." He pushes a strand of hair from my face, tucking it behind my ear. "You're so beautiful. Why don't you see that?" I shrug and he places his hands on my shoulders. "You, Fallyn, are incredibly beautiful and sexy. I want you to see what I see and what other men with a pulse see. You have the most sexy bedroom eyes and your smile is intoxicating. You have an amazing body, a body that men dream about. You're funny and outgoing and you have the cutest laugh." I try to look away, but he stops me. "Don't turn away, please."

"Why not?"

"Because," he moves closer to me, "one day, I hope to see you naked." A wicked smirk comes on his face and all of my senses skyrocket. The ache between my thighs goes into hyper drive and I swear I think I'm panting.

"You can't say those things to me."

"Why not?" He strokes my cheek down to my arm. I shiver to his touch and flutter my eyes closed. "One day..." He leans in and lightly kisses my lips. "Come take a walk with me on the beach."

"Okay," I breathlessly answer.

When we get to the beach, Jensen and I walk in silence near the shore. It's dark out, almost nine in the evening, but it's nice to walk with him. Our hands are constantly brushing against one another and I love how it feels. I wish he would take my hand and entwine his fingers with mine. But I know it can't happen now. He needs time to mourn over his breakup. Yet I can't stop looking and admiring his body. He carries himself in such a confident way, and even though he's broken over Lisa, he doesn't let it show. The way he conducts himself, taking charge and opening himself up, knowing how strong he is, is just so sexy. Everything about him screams sex. Even his voice. It's deep, but not creeper deep; sort of like the sexy

Vision of Hope

bedroom voice that you like to hear after making passionate love.

Thoughts about us making love nearly make me fall to my knees. I will myself to calm down and remind myself that Jensen won't go for a fat girl.

"What's on your mind?"

"Nothing," I answer, keeping my eyes straight ahead. Even though I know he's looking at me, I keep my eyes forward. If I stop and look at him, I'll fall apart, and I don't want that.

"You know you can talk to me, Fallyn. What's on your mind?"

"Nothing."

"Well, I think you're lying to me and I think you're letting the words of my ex get to you. She's nothing. What she said shouldn't touch you. Her venom is hers alone. Don't let it eat away at you."

"I'm really tired, Jensen. Can you take me home?" I don't want to stand here and hear more of his words. I know that I'm fat and I don't want to listen to him. I'll never be with a man like Jensen. I need to focus on my career and think about my life and make changes to ensure I'll lose weight and look and feel better.

Even though I really like Jensen.

Fuck.

Chapter 25
Jensen

Fallyn's been avoiding me since our walk on the beach. She's been dodging my texts and tells me she can't meet for lunch. Whenever I try to visit her on the floor, I'm told she's working the third shift. I get why she's staying away from me, but this ends today.

Finishing up the work in my office, I walk to my car, get in, and speed to her house. I'm not sure what I'm going to say, but whatever it is, she's going to listen and not say a word.

Pulling into her driveway, I see Isaac coming out of the house. "Hey, man!" He waves to me.

"Hey. Is Fallyn up?"

"Yeah, she's getting ready for work. Just go in." I smirk and tell him I'll talk to him later. Walking into her house, I quietly shut the door. I hear her singing and walk down the hall to her bedroom. She's wrapped in a towel, singing and dancing to "Blurred Lines" by Robin Thicke. I lean against the doorframe and watch her dance, shaking her ass and raising her hands in the air. Damn, I hope that towel falls off.

When she's done singing, I clap my hands together and see her body freeze. Walking into her room, I stand behind her, placing my hands on her bare shoulders. My lips softly brush the side of her head. A little gasp leaves her lips. My hands massage her tight shoulders and soon she's melting to my touch. Neither of us has said anything yet, and I'm not sure what to say. For the first time, my mind is blank. But the vision of her in this towel, dancing and singing, will stay with

Vision of Hope

me for a long time. Just standing here behind her is taking everything in me not to rip off the towel and cherish every inch of her luscious body.

Yelling at myself to calm down, I slightly walk backwards and watch her turn around to face me.

"What are you doing here?"

"I wanted to talk to you," I tell her.

"For what?"

My eyes go to her lips and my desire to kiss her again consumes me. My mind reels with everything I want to say and do to her. But then I remember my recent break up with Lisa and figure kissing her again, even being in the room with her, might be too soon. I don't need her thinking she's a rebound. She's far from that. I'm falling for this incredibly sexy woman in front of me and I want her to know that. I also want to take my time so that there aren't any doubts between us.

"I want to know why you're avoiding me. I know I didn't do anything wrong and it's bothering me that we're not hanging out like we used to." I see her thinking. "Stop thinking and tell me what's going on in your head!"

Her hands go around the towel. She's holding on to it, afraid it'll fall off. "The kiss is bothering me! What Lisa said to me is bothering me. I know that I'm not skinny and, when I think of you and her, it makes me realize that she's right. Nothing makes sense to me right now. I'm so lost and confused. I don't know what to do."

"Then talk to me. I want to know what's going on in your pretty head."

Fallyn turns around and sits on the ledge by her window. Her leg bounces and she bites her nails. "There's a lot going through my head, especially what Lisa said."

"What the fuck are you talking about?" The muscles in my arms flex and my eyes hold a cold stare. If I could have pushed Lisa out of my house that day, I would have. My pulse speeds and my body tenses. There's no way she can believe the vicious words from Lisa. "I know that you are not that stupid to believe her."

"Are you calling me stupid?"

"Only if you believe her," I fume. "If you're so dumb to believe that, then you're blind because you have no idea how people see you. I've told you this before how unbelievably sexy you are and, right now, all I want to do is rip that damn fucking towel off and throw you on your bed and spread you wide open so I can make you call out my name." She gasps and backs away from me. Good. Walking closer to her, I bring my hands to her face, caressing her, making her feel my desire for her. "I think I've made it clear that I want you. But I'm going to take my time because you need to realize that I'm falling for you and you are not a rebound."

"You have made it clear and it makes me happy to hear it, but I need to make sure that I'm not a rebound. I have so much going on and I need you to understand. Brody was the only man I've ever loved and been with. Moving on is hard and, even though I know he's not coming back, it still doesn't make it easy."

"I get it." I lean in and kiss her forehead. "I get it."

"It's hard," she whispers. "And I want to see where this can go between us, but we both have to be sure."

"I know. But do me a favor?"

"Yeah?"

"Stop killing yourself with these diets and working out. You're beautiful as you are. Being skinny doesn't mean you're instantly beautiful."

"Then you need to do me a favor," she quietly says.

"Of course."

"Don't rush me. Let *me* come to you."

I breathed a sigh. "I'll catch you when you're ready."

Vision of Hope

"So you're really falling for me?" I nod. "I am too." Her face blushes and it's the cutest thing I've seen.

"What happens now?"

"Well, now, I have to get ready for work, but I think maybe we can start taking it slow and get to know each other more."

"Sounds good." I kiss her forehead and bring her into my arms. I can be patient and wait until we're both ready. Fallyn's the type of woman you wait for. Her wholesome heart and caring personality, added to her beautiful soul, is something you don't find every day. The wait will be worth it and I'll treasure each moment until I can call her mine.

* * * * *

Of course, as things start with Fallyn, I'm backed into a corner and flooded with work at the hospital. I've been spending my nights and weekends with paper and revising documents. This isn't how I wanted to spend my time, but I tell myself this is what I wanted and what I've earned.

A knock on my front door brings me away from my computer. Getting up from the couch, I walk to the front door and see a beautiful Fallyn on the other side.

"Why, hello," she says, walking in and making her way into my kitchen. I notice the bags in her hands and wonder what she's up to. "So I know you've been super busy with work and I know you haven't been eating well, so I decided to come over and make you dinner. Do you object?"

"Absolutely not," I tell her. "Can I get you anything?"

"Nope. Finish what you're working on and, in about an hour, we'll eat and you can take a much needed break."

I sit back down and position myself so that I'm facing her. Watching her move freely in my kitchen, opening my cabinets, taking out the ingredients she needs for whatever she's making, is comforting. But seeing her like this is making me wonder. It's bringing back memories of when she told me about Brody and I can't help but wonder if she's going to allow herself to move on.

I don't want to think that she won't give herself another chance to love. The thought of her being alone makes me sick. I know she's falling for me like I have for her, but how can I make her see we can start something now?

"Come and eat!" I get up and walk to the dining room and see Fallyn's gone all out. In the middle of the table, there's a basket of bread with various dipping oils and butter, a salad bowl with caprese salad, and she's made a shrimp dish with mixed vegetables and quinoa.

"This looks and smells great." I rush over to give her a soft kiss on the cheek and pull out her chair. "Sit down, please."

"Thank you."

I take my seat on the other side of the table, wishing she'd have seated us next to one another. Looking at her, through the candles, I think she's perfect. The natural look she has is sexy. I've seen her wear makeup before, but this is the Fallyn I like.

"Thank you again for making me dinner. Everything looks amazing. You can come cook me dinner anytime you want, but next time, I'm going to cook for you."

"Maybe we can cook together?" she asks me. A blush spreads across her face and I can't help but smile.

"I'd like that."

I see Fallyn finally relax and a smile on her face. Her smile's contagious and soon I'm sitting here like a lovesick fool, watching her and waiting for her to say *I'm ready.* I want her to be ready, on her own.

After dinner, I have her relax in the living room with a glass of wine. Quickly, I clean the dishes and wipe down the counters. I didn't have to clean too much. Fallyn cleaned as she cooked.

Grabbing a glass of wine for myself, I join her on the couch. "Thank you again for dinner. I needed that tonight."

"You've been working so much lately and it's the least I can do. I make you get up early to go running and you've changed your entire schedule for me."

"I'd do it all over again."

I look outside and notice the clear skies. Putting down my wine glass and hers, I take her hand in mine and lead her outside to my deck. She follows my lead when I sit down and lie on my back.

"What are we doing?"

"Relaxing. We're ignoring everything around us and taking in the beauty of nature."

She's quiet and looks at me, but then turns her head up. I'm not sure how long we're out here for. The silence between us is nice. Her hand is next to mine and I want to feel it back in mine. The words *friend* and *slow down* hit me. Any contact with her will be worth it. Anything with her will be worth it. Looking at Fallyn gives me hope. I'm not sure what kind of hope, but whatever it is will be worth it.

"What are you thinking about?"

You.

"Being outside and finally not allowing myself to think about work. What about you?"

"Oh." The tone in her voice seems sad and she says it with a sigh of defeat. "Just things."

"What kind of things?"

"Can someone's heart hold two people?" I notice her hand inch to mine. "How do you know it's okay?"

"You feel it." I grab her hand and bring it to my lips. When I lightly kiss her hand, her eyes find mine and she doesn't pull away. "And I was thinking about you when you asked me."

"Then why didn't you tell me?"

"Because I don't know where your head is. I want to know what you're feeling and how you're feeling. I know this is going fast. You're the one on my mind. You're the one I want to be with." I sit up, her hand still in mine. Our eyes connect and I refuse to look away. "You're who I want to be with."

"I know," she says, sitting up and leaning in to kiss my lips. "Just give me time."

"Okay."

* * * * *

She's been spending more time with me at my house. I like having her here, doing things like cooking, watching TV, or relaxing on the couch and talking. The feelings I have for her are growing and I'm falling fast.

My phone vibrates on the counter and I pick it up.

Lisa: *Seriously, can we talk?*

Me: *There's nothing to talk about. I don't know why you're still trying to talk to me.*

Lisa: *Because I still fucking love you!*

Me: *Love? No, Lisa, you thought you loved me. If you loved me, then you wouldn't have cheated on me.*

Lisa: *It was a mistake!*

Me: *I'm done, Lisa.*

Shoving my phone in my pocket, I hear the chair pull out and shuffling from behind me. When I turn around, Fallyn's leaning on the counter with a smile on her face. Her blue eyes are bright and her hair is tied to the side.

"You look really pretty."

She blushes with my compliment. "Thank you. So do you need help with anything?"

"Nope. Go relax in the living room and when I'm done cooking, I'll come get you."

Vision of Hope

"Okay." She hops down from the chair and walks away. Before she leaves the kitchen, she turns her head back to me. "You look hot today." She winks and leaves me standing in my kitchen, wanting her.

The conversation is light during dinner. I look at her and watch as she swirls the pasta on her fork. When I reach out to touch her hand, she freezes and looks at me. There are so many things I want to ask her and so much I have to hold back.

"Fallyn?"

She looks up. "Yes?"

"I'm glad you're here with me tonight." I attempt a smile and to touch her hand again, but see the hesitation and fear in her eyes. It's like whenever we take two steps forward, we end up taking five steps back.

"I like being here with you." Her tone is unsure and soft. As soon as the words leave her beautiful lips, she looks back down at her food. Every ounce of me is holding back from holding her in my arms. It's all I want. I want to take this beautifully broken woman in my arms and tell her everything will be okay. I want to tell her it's okay to move on and she'll never have to wonder about or question my devotion for her.

What if she'll never be ready and we stay just friends?

The question makes my stomach turn. It's a possibility that she won't allow herself to be happy. When Jamie died, I grieved for her death, but grieved for Emma. I let her go as soon as her deception came to light. I get that my situation is different from hers, and I want to understand where she's coming from. Thinking about how she feels hurts my heart, and I want to be the one to heal her heart.

After dinner and two bottles of wine later, Fallyn gets up and heads to the kitchen. I watch her move and wonder what she's doing.

"Fallyn?"

She hurries up and looks for her things. I rub the back of my neck, trying to think about why she could be leaving when we've had a great night so far.

"I need to go home."

"And why's that?"

Her eyes widen and she shakes her head. "I don't trust myself here with you."

I stare at her. "You've lost me. What's going on with you? We've been having dinner at my house and you stay here with me until much later. I'm not pushing you to do anything."

"I know."

"So what's the problem? Why can't you trust yourself around me?" At this point, I don't mean to sound upset or angry. Her back and forth with her feelings doesn't make sense.

"I can't let you in to break my heart. I can't allow you to see me for who I am. I'm still dealing with Brody's death and not having a family. I have a lot of baggage and issues. It's not right for me to move on so soon." She's looking at the wall and refuses to meet my gaze. I'm studying her, watching her move her lips as she talks and the way she's sitting near me. She's fighting this and fighting us.

"You keep saying I'm going to hurt you and you assume that I will. What the hell have I done to make you think that? I'm being respectful and trying to be your friend." I walk closer to her, touching her shoulders, feeling her body tremble to my touch. "Help me understand."

"I don't want you to waste your time with me. I don't want to do something that'll hurt you or hurt our friendship. It means too much to me."

"So now you're scared of hurting me?" My tone is harsh. I don't mean to be rude, but she's confusing the fuck out of me.

"Well, I don't know."

Vision of Hope

I cross my arms and stare at her. "Tell me what you want," I slowly say, enunciating each word. "You tell me not to rush you and I'm not. Then you want to run away. If you don't know what you want, why are you here?"

She stands up and stands close to me. "I'm here because I want to be here. I'm here because we're friends and I like being with you. It's fun and there's no pressure."

"Funny. Usually, when people want to be near the person they're falling for, they aren't acting like this."

"You're being an asshole, Jensen."

"And you're confusing the fuck outta me!" I turn away, afraid to look at her. "I get it. I get that you miss him and that you're scared of moving on, but I have feelings too. And you're treating me as if I'm gonna fuck you and leave you."

Her hand rests on my shoulder, giving it a squeeze. She doesn't say anything and neither do I. My gut clenches and something sprints through my body, pushing down to my legs, making me turn away and pull her in my arms. She fights, but I fight harder. I know I want to give myself more time and be fair. After spending time with her as much as I do, I'm being unfair to myself. Deep down, the thought of loving Lisa and getting her back makes me sick. I can never trust her and I'm at the point in my life where I need more.

"We all have issues. I know what happened to you and you know me. And why would you think I would break your heart?"

"Because *if* you decide to date me, you'll see I have too many issues, then leave me to find someone else."

Now I'm pissed. She obviously doesn't know me. "We keep going round and round. Don't worry about me breaking your heart because you don't have faith in me, so what's the point?" I walk away, leaving her in the kitchen. I don't know what else to say. Heading into my bedroom, I close the door and fall to my bed. I think about what she said and want to shake her for thinking that. I've never given her any doubt, so why is she starting now?

In a matter of seconds, the night changes. The back and forth games we're playing are pissing me off. I like her and I know damn well she likes me. She has baggage and so do I. Maybe I'm fooling myself and this is a sign or some shit. Maybe I'm over thinking and need to take a step back. When she's around me, I can't think clearly. There's a pull to her and I don't want to let go. I don't want to cut the tie because I want her to push so I can pull harder.

A little over an hour passes with me and my thoughts before I head back out. Fallyn's sleeping on the couch and little soft snores are escaping her soft lips. Her shiny blonde hair covers parts of her face. I take a moment and stare at her, taking her in, memorizing her every feature.

I lift her in my arms and bring her to my bedroom. I ignore how soft her body feels against mine and how I wish she would let go of her insecurities and realize how good we can be together.

Kissing her forehead, I bring the blanket to her chin and leave my bedroom and head to the guest bedroom. Everything in me is screaming to run to her and hold her throughout the night. I want to hear her breathe and know what she's dreaming about. I want to feel her in my arms and never let go. This is what she's doing to me and I want more. I need more. Now to figure out how to get her to be mine.

The next morning, the smell of bacon and eggs assault my senses. Rising quickly out of bed, I walk out into the kitchen and find Fallyn by the stove, cooking.

"Morning."

She turns and her face turns bright pink. "Hi," she quietly says.

"Did you sleep well?"

"I did. And you?"

Vision of Hope

"Yeah."

Okay, enough with the small talk. "So do you mind telling me what was up with yesterday?"

"Do you wanna know the truth?"

I nod. "That'll be helpful."

"You know I'm scared, but the real reasons I'm scared are because I don't want people looking at me badly for moving on so fast and I don't want to forget Brody and our lives together. He just passed away six, almost seven, months ago. I feel like I need more time, even though I do like you a lot."

Shocked isn't the word. I get her fears of being judged and what people will say. I'd never let any negative words hurt her. Just like I'd never let her forget about the man she loves. As much as it pains me to admit it, I want to keep his memory alive and learn more about Brody.

Slowly walking around the counter and to her side, I stroke her arm with my fingers and tilt her head towards me. "I will *never* allow anyone to hurt you with their judgments and I will *never* allow you to forget Brody. I want to know more about him, Fallyn. Will you tell me?"

Her eyes widen and her jaw drops. Placing my fingers under her chin, I close her mouth for her, trying so hard not to laugh. Her hand touches her chest and then mine.

"You're beautiful," she softly speaks with adoration and surprise.

"I told you everything and I want you to believe me." I pause and look at her. I have to be careful when I ask her certain questions, hoping I don't trigger her impulse to run. "Do you think you made a mistake, thinking you can push me away with your insecurities?"

Without faltering, she answers, "Yes."

"Do you think maybe you should give us a chance?" Her body tenses and she continues to look at me. "Take your time."

"That's all I think about. You are all I think about. Even when I don't want to, you're still on my mind. I miss you when we're not together and I've been trying so hard to think of you as a friend, but I can't. And then you kissed me and it's confusing me. I like you so much, but are you over Lisa?"

"Yes."

"How can you be so sure?"

She fidgets and sways side to side. I keep my eyes on her and wait for her to look at me again. I need her to look at me when I talk to her. "When I look at you, I see you. I don't see Lisa or anyone else." I pull out my phone and hand it to her. "Here; look at my messages to Lisa."

"No. I don't want to. I want to trust you."

I place the phone in her hand and kiss her forehead. "Just read them, please." I turn and walk away so she can have privacy. I'm serious about wanting to make her mine and I'll do anything I can to make it happen.

Sitting on the couch, I turn on the TV and watch the news. Minutes pass and Fallyn sits down next to me, resting her hand on my upper thigh.

"I don't want to be a rebound. I want to be someone you want, not someone that you sleep with and forget because your heart's broken."

"You're right." Her head shoots up and my eyes meet hers. My hands caress her face and she leans in to my touch, wanting so much more and kicking myself for not thinking about her feelings. "You're a beautiful woman, Fallyn. You deserve to be swept off your feet and showered with love and adoration. You're not someone I could sleep with and then forget." She doesn't say anything, and that's fine. I need her to listen to my words and take it all in. The more walls she has, the more I'm willing to break down each one.

Chapter 26
Fallyn

Jensen touches my hand, stroking it lightly, sending shivers down my body. What the hell? "Having you here, right now, means the world to me, Fallyn. You've been a great friend and I appreciate everything you've been doing." He pauses, keeping his stare strong and intense. I lick my lips without realizing it. Shit, he's really close. "I don't know what I would do without you." His eyes fall on my lips as he comes in closer and I let him. As his lips touch mine, a fire inside me ignites. I want him. I want to feel him against me. His tongue invades my mouth. My hands wrap around his neck, bringing him closer to me.

The promise of this kiss fills me with hope of a chance to be happy. For so long, I've been alone, and here I am in the arms of Jensen and I don't want to leave. It's an amazing feeling to feel wanted again.

Jensen pulls away, still looking at me with warmth in his eyes. "I want you. I want more than to be your friend," he whispers.

"When you say you want me…"

"I'm not saying in that way." He pauses and smirks. "Yet. I want to do things differently. You make me feel good, and I don't want to rush into things. I can wait."

The way his words sink into me causes my heart to skip a beat. It seems so sweet and innocent, just like him. *Slow*. We both need to take things slow. Both of our hearts are vulnerable. There's no reason to rush things. Honestly, I'm scared to jump into another relationship. Having only been with Brody, I'm scared that I'm not experienced enough in the relationship world to be with Jensen.

These questions flood my mind, driving me crazy and giving me doubts. Right now, in this moment, I think I can only give him friendship.

"I need to get going. I have to work tonight."

"I don't like you working overnights." He pulls me to his body and we fall on his couch. Bursts of laughter spill from both of us. I try moving out of his arms and lap, but he keeps me in place. "You're not going anywhere. I love feeling you in my arms."

I don't fight back. Instead, I lean into him and we sit in a peaceful silence, enjoying the calmness and each other.

* * * * *

It's three in the morning when I leave the hospital. I'm exhausted, mentally, physically and emotionally, and just want my bed. My mind has been full of thoughts all night. Every reason I have to stay away from Jensen, I can come up with a reason to give in.

I've been texting Isaac and he thinks I need to move on. The hardest thing about letting go is letting go, if that makes sense. I've been holding on to his memories and I'm tired. I'm tired of trying to make sense of what happened and why Brody had to die. The answer will never come to me and it's not fair to sit here and always wonder. I don't want this chance to run from me. Maybe I'm looking for someone to give me the *okay* to move on.

The fear of what people think comes to the front of my mind. Will people think I'm a whore for moving on so fast? Does moving on mean you've stopping loving the person you're moving on from?

Vision of Hope

When I get in my car, my phone rings. Taking it out, I see a text from Jensen.

Jensen: *I wish you were here..Please change your mind and come back tonight*

I want to say *yes I'll be right over* and fall asleep in his arms. "Damn you, Brody. I need a sign or something. I know people are telling me to move on, but I need you to be okay with it. Can you please come down from Heaven and be next to me?" A sigh escapes my lips. I can't answer Jensen yet.

My phone rings and I look to see that the call is coming from Isaac.

"Hey," I answer.

"You're thinking, aren't you?" I look around the parking lot from my car, but it's just me. "Fallyn, what's wrong?"

"Jensen wants me and he likes me. I feel the same, but it's like I don't know what to do. He just broke up with Lisa..."

"Who cheated on him," he interrupts me. "He's not going back to her."

"Well, then there's Brody. The man I love and was supposed to spend my life with."

He breathes into the phone and I hear him moving around. "I get it. I miss my brother every fucking day, but you know him. He wouldn't want you to live your life like this. There's nothing that can bring back Brody." Isaac pauses, giving both of us a chance to take in what he said. "I'm sorry. I know that was mean and heartless, but you know it's true. I truly think Jensen's a great guy and he cares about you. I see the way he looks at you and you've been in a better mood since he's been in your life. You know, Mom and I think he will make you happy. . Don't pause your life because you don't think it's right. You've been grieving over Brody for a while. There's no rule that says you can only move on after a certain time period. If you have someone great in your life, then why don't you do something about it?"

"I'm going to go over to his house and be happy. You're right. If I don't do anything about it, then I'll never know." Saying out loud what I've been feeling gives me the confidence I need. It's out there and I can't take it back.

Isaac tells me to have fun and we say bye before I send Jensen a text message.

Me: =) okay.

Reaching his house, I see him on the porch, waiting for me. I walk a little faster and jump into his arms.

"I missed you." He holds me tight, as if he doesn't want to let me go, and we stand there, soaking in every moment.

"You saw me a few hours ago."

"And?" He smells my hair and brings me inside. He nuzzles my neck, and holds me close to him.

"We need to talk," I finally let out. "Please?" We sit down on the couch in his living room. Pulling my legs underneath me, I rest against the cushion and repeat what I want to say in my head. "I like you, Jensen. And I want to be with you," I start to say, carefully talking so I don't hurt his feelings or mine. "I know we agreed to be friends and take things slow."

"We did."

"But I'm ready. I'm ready to fall into your arms and let you hold me. I'm ready for you to see me, all of me, and create a life with you. If that's what you still want?"

Jensen pulls me into his arms, crashing his lips to mine, as I dig my fingers in his hair. His hands roam my back and down to my ass, picking me up and placing me on his lap. This moment, right here, right now, is perfect. I feel his erection in my center and immediately pull back.

"I'm sorry." He kisses me again. "Slow." I nod and kiss his cheek. When I stand up in front of him, he takes my hand and we walk upstairs together.

He leads me to his bathroom and I notice his clothes on the counter. "You can wear my clothes tonight."

Vision of Hope

"Thank you. I usually have clothes with me. Just to let you know if your clothes are comfortable you aren't getting it back!"

He laughs and kisses the tip of my nose. "Go shower and get ready for bed so I can hold you in my arms all night."

"Okay." I smile and kiss him before walking into this giant bathroom. Closing the door, I lean against the wall and cover my face with my hands. Finally catching my breath, I take in his beautiful bathroom. There's a large porcelain tub under the large window. His walk-in shower is made of gray and black tiles with a large showerhead and shower jets on the side.

Taking off my clothes, I step in and let the water fall over my body. I stand below the showerhead and tilt my head back, allowing the water to freely flow from my hair to the floor.

Turning off the water I wrap the towel around my body and change into his clothes. Yep he's not getting these back.

Drying my hair as much as I can I head out of the bathroom and head down the hall to his room. Walking in I look at him as he's sitting on his bed, without a shirt, and reading a book.

"Hi."

"Hi." He looks at me and smiles, patting the bed next to him. "You're so beautiful." Sitting down next to him, I place my head on his shoulder and try to read what he's reading. His hand is resting on my thigh and I let out a sigh, loving this moment with him. "When we first met, I didn't think anything of you. I was so wrapped up in my life with Lisa and making her happy. You and I became friends and you became an important person in my life. I don't know how I would have handled this on my own. Even though my heart hurts, you being here with me is making it better. I feel like there's life being breathed back into me and it's because of you, Fallyn. You're bringing me back to life."

I blink my eyes a few times and gently kiss his lips. My God, this man is so beautifully broken and scared and I am too, but together, we can overcome our fears.

"I'm going to make mistakes. I'm not perfect."

"Neither am I, Jensen. I want to be imperfect with you."

"Let's be imperfect," he kisses me, "together." He kisses me again and I relax in his arms. My eyes feel heavy and just as I'm about to fall asleep I hear him tell me something. "Don't leave me."

"I love seeing you smile."

I turn around and see Brody sitting on a bench under a tree. He looks so handsome. "Brody?"

"Hi beautiful. I love seeing you happy."

He's holding his hand out to me. I'm running as fast as I can, yelling for him to stop. There's a smile on his face and he gets up to walk away, still facing me.

"Brody! Stop!," I cry out. My legs start to give out, but I keep going.

"Let Jensen in," Brody says. "I want you to be happy, Angel. I will always love you and have your heart. You have enough room for both of us. Don't pause your life because I'm gone. You still have a long time. Don't worry, though. I'll be here waiting for you."

The tunnel gets darker. There's a force holding me back. No matter what I do, I can't reach him. "Stop! Please stop! Come back!"

"Fallyn!" My body is shaking. Quickly, I open my eyes and see the worried look on his face. "Are you okay?" He brings me up into his arms as my restless body lies limp, and I don't have the energy to hug him back. "Where'd you go?" he whispers in my hair.

I don't answer.

I can't answer.

"I'm here. I'm here," he repeats.

Vision of Hope

I hear him telling me he'll be here. I want him to know how much I love hearing it. But part of me is still with Brody. This isn't fair to Jensen. Here I am, still holding on to the ghosts of my past and I can't move on. Even when I think I can, I can't. "Maybe I should go home."

"No. Don't go home. I'll do whatever you need. What do you need?"

I want him. I want to be happy and I'm trying so hard. Everyone deserves a chance to be happy and I do too. I know Brody is gone and he's not coming back. I know that he'd want me to move on and I'm trying to tell myself that too. "Tell me it's going to be okay."

Jensen lays me down and pulls me to his chest, "As long as we try and talk to each other everything will be okay." My back rests against him and his arm wraps around my waist. I breathe in and out, telling myself this is okay.

"Sleep," he whispers. "Tomorrow's a new day."

The next morning, we wake up at the same time. Our bodies are tangled together and I like knowing that I can sleep with him holding me.

"Okay, well, I'm up and it looks like you are too. Wanna go for a run with me?"

"Sure." I smile, realizing I don't have clothes. "You didn't bring my workout clothes?"

"We'll drive to your place and you can change." He smiles, and what a smile. We get out of bed and he heads to the bathroom. When the door closes, I pick up my phone and call her.

"Morning, Fallyn!"

"Hi," I pause, not sure if I should call her this, "Mom."

"Oh, sweetie. I know it's hard, but you can still call me Mom. Is that okay?"

"Yeah." I nod my head. "It is. I wanted to call you and let you know I'm okay and hear you tell me it's okay."

"Fallyn," she starts to say, "I already told Isaac so I'm going to tell you now. It's okay."

" I feel like if I do, then I'm cheating on him and everything we stood for."

"Honey, don't think that. I know it hurts to remember he's not coming back." She pauses and I hear her breathing steadily increase. It's hard to talk about because his death is still raw in our hearts. "Everyone wants you to be happy, honey and that's good. It's okay to meet someone and get close to him."

"Really? I mean, I know Brody said you guys talked and everything. I guess I needed to hear it from you."

"Yes. It's okay. I want you to move on. We all do."

We talk for a few more minutes about the weather and what's going on around town. I love talking to her and getting her advice.

"Thanks again for talking with me, Julie."

"Anytime. You can always call me."

"Send Phil my love and tell Isaac I miss him and want him to come back!"

"Will do, honey. Love you."

"Love you too." I disconnect the call and rest the phone on my knee, still looking out the window.

"Do you feel better?"

I turn around and Jensen's behind me with wet hair. My eyes travel down his amazing body and I'm literally counting his abs and, wow, his V. I stop breathing and watch as he puts on a long-sleeved shirt. His muscles move with him and I swear it's like my own private Magic Jensen show. I can sit here for hours and watch him.

"Are you done raping me with your eyes?" He cocks his brow.

My heart immediately stops beating and my face turns bright red.

"Raping you? With my eyes? No! Shut up!"

"Really? Because I saw you licking your lips and your breathing became quick." He moves closer to me. "I might have liked you checking me out." He winks. "But do you feel better?"

I nod and smile. "Yeah, I do." I bring his face to mine and kiss his lips. "I feel a lot better." Jensen opens his car door for me and then climbs in. Starting his car, he zooms out of the neighborhood and drives to my house.

Night comes too quickly and I'm wrapped in Jensen's arms. I keep thinking about what Julie said to me and what Isaac told me. It's okay for me to move on and it's okay to be happy again. I have to tell myself this or else I won't be able to be okay.

Grabbing the remote from his hands, I turn off the TV and take his hand in mine. Our touch is light and soft. He casts his gaze to me and neither of us talk. Taking him to his room, I stand in front of him and slowly strip out of my shorts and tank. In front of him in my bra and panties, I feel okay, but nervous. I haven't been naked in front of a man since Brody.

"Fallyn." His hoarse whisper lingers in the air. "What are you doing?"

"I want you." I walk to him and stroke his arm up and down. My eyes find his and his head is tilted back. "I'm ready."

"Are you sure? It's okay. I can wait."

"I want you, Jensen."

"I've dreamed of this moment with you for so long. I don't want to rush."

Inside, I'm throwing my hands in the air. He's been fantasizing about me and I love how close he wants me to be with him. His lips touch my neck and his hands move their way down my body. I shiver from his touch and crave more.

He lifts me up and I wrap my legs around his waist. "I'm going to make love to you tonight, Fallyn."

"Please do," I whimper, holding him tight.

Laying me down on his bed, he flutters my body with kisses and slowly takes off my panties. "Before I feel inside of you, I need to taste you." He licks his lips and I can't help but let out a moan. Here I am, nearly naked on his bed, waiting to feel him, and everything seems right. There's nothing holding me back. For the first time, I feel ready and needy.

He kneels down before me and spreads my legs. Tenderly, he kisses my inner thighs and takes his time, causing my body to shake. I arch my back from the bed and moan, letting him know how badly I want his tongue on me. Right before I feel his tongue, his finger slides up and down my center. Then, he slides his tongue over me. His tongue and mouth masterfully move, sucking and licking my clit. The pleasure he's giving me is nothing I've ever experienced.

His tongue moves faster and, in seconds, I'm screaming his name. My hips thrust into his mouth and my hands are in his hair. I don't want him to stop. I love him licking and sucking me.

Immediately, he pulls away and looks at me with dark eyes. "Are you ready for me?"

My eyes go directly to his erection and now it's my turn to lick my lips. He seems so big and I can't wait to feel him inside of me.

"I want you, Jensen."

"Condom?" he whispers, reaching into his drawer.

I shake my head. "I'm on the pill, and I've only been with Brody."

"I've always used a condom with Lisa. After Jamie, I got tested, and I'm clean. I've never had sex without a condom before." He smirks. "I'm glad my first time will be with you."

I get up from the bed and take off my bra, letting the straps fall down my arm and to the bedroom floor. Jensen takes in my naked body and grabs my hands, bringing me to him.

Vision of Hope

"Do you feel what you're doing to me?"

"Yes."

His hands unbutton his jeans and soon he's naked too. My eyes go to his cock and I let out a gasp. Holy shit, how is he going to fit inside me?

"Shhhh," he says, picking me up and bringing me back to his bed. He lays me down on top of his pillows and looks at me. "You're so beautiful."

"You are too." I let out a giggle, making him smile. His hands are on my knees, slowly opening as he pushes himself into me. I feel his dick barely enter me and see his eyes rolling back. "Don't stop."

"It feels so fucking good." He slowly enters me again and slides out. This is going to kill me.

"Jensen," I moan.

"Baby, you're going to have to give me some time. I'm going to fucking blow if I rush this."

He leans down and kisses me, stroking my bottom lip with his tongue. I open my mouth and let his tongue invade my mouth with such passion and sweetness. The kiss drowns me and soon he's inside me. I move my head to the side, gripping his ass, screaming for more. He goes faster, entering me deeper until he's all the way in.

"Fuck," he hisses. "Fuck, Fallyn. You're so tight." Our lips meet again. The kiss, our lovemaking, is heaven.

"Jensen! Jensen!" I feel my orgasm building up.

"Yes, Fallyn." He pumps faster and soon our orgasms sweep over us and the moans coming from us are explosive.

Jensen slowly pulls out of me and goes to the bathroom. When he comes out, he's wearing sweatpants and has a washcloth in his hands. He cleans me up and I let him. This is so sexy.

Tossing the washcloth in the corner, he comes on the bed and pulls me into his arms. "You're amazing."

"You are too," I sleepily whisper. "So amazing." My eyes fall closed and before I enter dream world, I swear I hear Jensen talk.

"Don't ever leave me, Fallyn. I'm falling in love with you."

Chapter 27

Jensen

Nicholas has invited us over for dinner tonight. It's been incredible spending time with Fallyn since we've been official. She spends most of her time at my house and, sometimes, I'll go over to her house.

For the past few days, she's had a glow about her and I love seeing her smile, but then she goes into a trance. There is nothing I can do to make her stop missing Brody. At night, she'll get a lost look in her eyes. I won't pull her out of it. This is something she needs to do on her own. I understand her sadness. When I lost Jamie, I was sad, but part of me was relieved. Even though she did the most evil things, her heart was still there and she allowed me to see her heart and who she was. But her anger took over and killed her.

"Fallyn!" I call upstairs for her. "Are you ready? We have to be there now."

"I'm coming!" she yells back and I shake my head. Lately, she's been taking longer to get ready. I miss the girl who only took fifteen minutes getting ready.

Pulling out the bottle of wine from my collection and the plate of baked goods made by Fallyn, I set both on the counter and wait for her to come down the stairs.

"I'm going to leave without you!"

"Shut up!" she screams and I hear her footsteps coming downstairs. One look at this beautiful woman and I'm about to fall face first. The soft green dress she's wearing ends a little above her knees. Her toned legs go on for miles with the brown wedges she has on. My God, she's fucking beautiful.

I look up and see that her straight blonde hair and her makeup are done. I'm about to tell Nicholas we aren't coming today. All I want to do is run my fingers through her hair and let her worries seep from her body to be replaced with my love.

"Come on, beautiful." I pass her the bottle of wine and take her hand. We walk out of my house together and I open the door for her. She slides in and, when I get in the car, she leans over and kisses my cheek.

My fingers entwine with hers. As we get closer to Nicholas and Karly's house, I see a car I don't recognize and my hand clenches the steering wheel. My phone vibrates and Fallyn picks it up.

"It's from Karly."

"Open the text."

"Lisa's here. I didn't know she was coming. Nicholas is pissed, but Stephen doesn't know what happened the last time she was in town. Do you want me to get her to leave?"

I look at Fallyn and her eyes meet mine. "I'll do whatever you want."

She shakes her head. "No, it's fine. I'm not afraid to be near her. I'm kinda upset that Stephen didn't tell us, though." Just as she finishes talking, her phone goes off along with mine. "It's Stephen. He said he's sorry that Lisa's over and he should've told her not to come along."

"Well, if you're okay with going, then we'll go. Just please don't let her words hurt you."

"I won't." She squeezes my hand and I park behind Stephen, ready to key his car.

We walk up the driveway and around to the back where the party is being held. Nicholas and Larry are at the grill and the girls are relaxing by the pool. Lisa's next to Stephen and his back is to us. It looks like he's talking to her and her head is down.

"Hey, guys," I announce, setting down the plate and taking the wine from Fallyn.

"Hey," the group says. Fallyn tugs on my arm and nods her head to where Lexi and Karly are.

I watch her walk over, pass Lisa, and sit down with them. Lisa's eyes find Fallyn and the daggers coming from her pisses me the fuck off.

"Stephen." I walk to him. "Hi, Lisa."

"Hey." She tries to hug me, but Stephen looks at her and she stops. "Good to see you."

"You too."

"Hey, man did you get my text?" I nod. "Alright. Let's grab a beer. Lisa, remember what I said."

"Okay," she says, looking at us, then towards the pool.

Stephen and I walk over to the grill and Larry hands me a shot. "You look like you need this, brother."

"You don't fucking know," I seethe and down the shot. "What the fuck is your sister doing here?"

"Man, I don't know. She's not supposed to be home until tomorrow, but she said she wanted to come home and she's here."

"There better not be any drama today, Stephen. I love you like a brother, but if I hear anything negative from her, she's out."

"I talked to her and she gets it," Stephen explains. "It'll be fine."

We talk about sports and work for a little before Lexi comes over to us. "You're not gonna be here for Thanksgiving?" She pouts.

"Huh?"

"Fallyn just told us she bought the both of you plane tickets to Montana. She said you're having Thanksgiving with

Brody's family." I look up and find her looking at me. I should be upset that we didn't talk about Thanksgiving, but given the circumstances, she probably said that to let Lisa know to back off.

"Yeah, I am heading there. Sorry for not saying anything."

The day goes by without any problems. We sit down and have dinner and I wonder where Emma and Sebastian are.

"With Nicholas' parents. They wanted them for the day so we said *yes*!" Karly laughs. "I love my kids, but oh my God, sometimes I need a break."

"Where's Kayden?" Lisa asks Lexi.

"With my parents too," Lexi answers matter-of-factly. "One night without Kayden will be heavenly."

"My son hates me," Larry says. "Every time I kiss Lexi or even come near her, he screams and throws a tantrum. How can a baby do that?"

The table erupts with laughing and nodding of agreement. I look at Fallyn and instantly see a baby bump on her. I have no idea where the fuck that image came from, but I'm okay with seeing her pregnant with my child. Maybe children.

"So, Fallyn, you look good. Have you been working out?"

All eyes are on Lisa. What the fuck is she doing?

Confidently, Fallyn answers her. "Sure am, Lisa. I've been working out with Jensen."

"What kind of question is that?" Karly snarls at Lisa.

"I was just asking, jeez. I didn't mean anything by that."

Stephen leans into Lisa and whispers something to her. I watch her reaction and then turn my head to Fallyn.

"Are you okay?"

She nods. "Yeah. And I'm sorry I didn't tell you about Montana. I hope that's okay?"

I kiss the tip of her nose. "Of course, baby. I'm excited to come with you."

Vision of Hope

"Me too." She smiles and continues her conversation with the group.

*****

Putting down a book I've been reading, I glance down at the incredible and sexy girl sleeping. I smile as I look at her.

Even though we've only been together for a short while, she's everything to me. Does that sound crazy? The way she makes me feel is different. Even with a broken heart, she didn't look the other way. She helped me through it and made me realize what love is. The idea of not being with her kills me. The idea of making her cry or disappointing her kills me. I'm whole again and it's because of Fallyn.

Turning off the light, I slide down and pull her against my body. She fits perfectly in my arms. Stroking her arm, lightly kissing the side of her head, I smile, thinking about making love to her. With her, it's not about fucking, but cherishing each other, memorizing each other, and making love. It wasn't rushed or hurried. I took my time making sure she fell apart while I was inside of her more than once. Hearing her moan my name, telling me how I made her feel, feeling her heartbeat against mine; in that moment, I fell in love with her. She's the air I breathe and all I want to do is take her in my arms and hold her forever.

"Jensen," she moans, taking my dick in her hands. Fuck, it feels good having her hand on me, stroking me up and down.

"Right here, baby. Right here."

She turns around, staring into my eyes while holding my dick tightly in her hand. Her soft hand feels fucking amazing. Pulling her on top of me, I help her slide down on me. I know we're both tired, but fuck, do I need her.

"Jensen," she moans, rocking back and forth. "This feels so good."

My hands touch her stomach and travel up to her breasts. Her body shudders against my touch. She rocks against me and I push her back a little. I rub her clit with my fingers and watch her throw her head back. Fuck, she's going to make me come soon.

The smell of her arousal hits me. I grab her hips, pumping into her fast and hard. Shit, this feels so good. "Fuck," I cry out as her muscles tighten around my dick. Feeling her, all of her, pushes my heart to the limits. When our bodies touch, a charge of life rushes through. It makes me lose control and I don't know how to breathe. I forget the basics when she's around.

Fallyn loses herself. She throws her head back, moaning and screaming for me to fuck her harder. Watching her fall apart sends me over the edge. I spill inside her and bring her lips to mine. "You're so beautiful," I whisper against her lips. "And you're mine."

She laughs and pushes herself off me. "Wow, that was amazing. But can we please sleep!"

"Fine." We kiss each other goodnight and I wrap my arms around her, pulling her close to my chest. "Sweet dreams, baby."

Waking up the next morning with her in my arms is something I'm never going to get used to. The simple act of holding her through the night, watching her sleep and hearing her breathing leaves me feeling speechless. The love I have for Fallyn is something I never felt, not even with Lisa. I want to tell her what's in my heart and to be honest I want to know if she's feeling the same way. Part of me is scared, while the other part is screaming for me to stop being a pussy and man the fuck up.

When her eyes open, she sees me looking at her and the sexiest grin comes on her face.

"I love waking up next to you. Can we do this forever and ever?"

Now Jensen. Now.

"If that's what you want, then that's what will happen."

"Yeah?" Her eyes light up and she kisses the tip of my nose.

Man the fuck up you damn pussy.

I sweep her hair from her eyes and meet her lips with mine. So gently I kiss her and place my hand on her cheek. "I love you, Fallyn." The words I've been holding onto easily slip from my lips. I'm afraid to look at her. I don't want her to run or leave me.

Pulling back I don't see fear or anger. The look on her face is priceless and I realize that taking this next step with her is a good thing. She shows me love and a smile on her face lets me know she's feeling the same way. "I love you too, Jensen."

"Thank you for being my best friend and helping me through the obstacles. Realizing I love you and hearing you say it back to me means the world to me. I know I sound extremely sappy now," she laughs, "But I mean it. Having you in my life means more to me than you'll ever know."

She touches my face and places her head on my chest. "I do know."

Pouring coffee for both of us, I adjust my tie, waiting for her to come out of the bedroom so we can head in to work together. My phone vibrates on the table. I pick it up and close my eyes, turning my head away.

"Is it Lisa?"

"Yeah, baby, it is."

Fallyn comes on the other side of the counter and picks up her cup of coffee. She takes a few sips, sighs, and looks at me. "Talk to her. She obviously needs you."

"I don't care what she needs." I place my hands on her shoulders, "She doesn't matter to me anymore. You matter to me."

"I know." She smiles. "And that's why I'm okay with you talking to her. She's probably not in a good place with everyone turning their backs on her. It's okay, babe." She kisses my cheek and walks out of the kitchen.

I know that she's telling me it's okay to talk to Lisa and be there for her. I get that she trusts me and it's nice, but I know what I have to do. Lisa isn't going to get in the middle of me and Fallyn. I know what she's trying to do and it won't work. She has Stephen. If she needs someone, she can go to him. Thinking about her pisses me off. She has no right to be in my head. She messed up and gave up what could have been. I need to be a better man and stop letting her come into my head. I'm about to throw my phone across the room and change my number when I see her smiling face and I'm calm. My breathing is back to normal and my heart slows down.

I'm not going to fuck this up with her. She deserves the world and all of me. I watch her get ready, feeling comfortable in my home. I think about the possibilities of the next step. She shares her house with Isaac, so I wonder if it'll be a problem to have her come live with me.

"Ready?"

I look up and see her by the front door. "Ready, babe."

* * * * *

The day goes by slower than it should. Fallyn's busy on her floor today, so we can't meet for lunch. After a few meetings this afternoon, I'm ready to head home. Finishing my last email I hear the door open and I hope it's Fallyn.

"Babe, I'll be done soon and then we can head out."

Vision of Hope

"Jensen." Her voice hits my ears, causing everything to stop. "I need to talk to you."

I take a deep breath and turn to look at her. "What, Lisa?"

Her lips start moving, but all I can think about is Fallyn. What will she think if she walks in and sees Lisa in my office? I don't want to give her the wrong impression.

"Are you even listening to me?"

I look up. "I'm sorry. What are you saying?"

"Are you waiting for someone?"

"I am. My *girlfriend.*"

"You don't have to be nasty about it, Jensen." When she says my name, I cringe. I'm about to tell her to leave when I see tears in her eyes. I should go to her and comfort her, then I see Fallyn's face. She's healing and moving on with me. I don't want to mess this up. I don't want to mess this up.

I stay at my desk, staring at her as she cries. I'm not going to fall for the games she's playing. She's unpredictable and I don't want to be caught up in her web of drama. This lasts for a few minutes. She doesn't look at me and keeps her head in her hands. Her shoulders tremble, but I stay at my desk. All I want is for her to leave so I can go back to the woman I love.

"I'm sorry, Jensen. If I could turn back time, I would," she says quietly, still crying and not able to look at me. "I know that you've moved on and you seem like you're doing well. It's just I can't let you go. Letting you go was the biggest mistake of my life. I know that the last time you saw me, we fought. I'm trying so hard to move on and be happy. If you can, I can too, right?" I don't respond. "I wish I realized what I had when we were together. God, Jensen. If only I could turn back time and go back to a few months ago. I still love you so much. Do you still love me?"

The question hits me. Lisa's going to be part of me for a while. I'm not that heartless, but the love of my life is waiting for me and I've made her wait for too long. I never thought I'd fall for someone this fast and hard. I never thought I'd call someone the love of my life when we've together for a few short months. But Fallyn is it for me. She's the one I want to be with and she's the one who'll grow old with me. One day, we'll be holding hands, sitting on the porch, watching our great grandkids playing in the yard. The sun will be setting and we'll call everyone to come inside. Our kids and their kids will be in the house, setting the dinner table. We'll look at our family and smile because it's been a great life.

"I can give you what you want now, Jensen. Before, I was selfish and wanted you all to myself. But I'll come back home and we'll be together. I can change. I can be the girl you fell in love with."

"But you can't. I've moved on, Lisa. This is something you'll have to accept. I love her and she deserves me to be honest and real. I'm not doing this with you. Please leave."

"I can't. I don't want to. I want us to try. Listen, I'm home for Thanksgiving break. Will I at least see you?"

"No. I'm going away with Fallyn." I love the idea of how strong she is and inviting me with her. I know this is a big step for her, letting me all the way in and introducing me to the other half of her life.

"Jensen! Can I please have your attention?"

"I'm sorry, Lisa."

"Please give us another chance. I'll be better. You don't throw away a love like ours."

"Exactly; you don't and you did. I did love you, Lisa, and I would have done anything for you, but when I started falling for Fallyn, something came alive in me. She makes it better. When I'm with her, all I can see is her. My heart beats for her and, when I think about my future, I think about her. You and I had our chance and a love that was great, but this is true love. This is the type of love you want forever. And Fallyn is my forever."

Vision of Hope

Lisa straightens her back and rolls her eyes. "Whatever. You'll come back to me and when you do, I'll make you beg me to come back. She's nothing and you'll realize that. Plus, since when do you like fat girls?"

Red. I see red. "Lisa, out of respect for Stephen, I'm not going to lose my shit on you. But you do *not* talk about Fallyn like that. Get out, Lisa. Now."

She gets up from the chair. "What?"

"Now. Lisa, get out. I need to leave and you need to get out of my office and do not come back. Do I make myself clear?"

Lisa huffs and rushes out of my office. I rub my eyes and let out a groan. When I open my eyes, I can't help the smile that forms on my face.

"I'm sorry that you have to deal with her."

"Don't be." I shake my head. "I want you to understand that what she says means nothing to me and it shouldn't hurt you." Picking up my briefcase, I round the corner of my desk and take this beautiful woman in my arms.

Her head rests on my chest and holds me tight. "I know."

Chapter 28
Fallyn

Jensen's away at a medical conference, and I'm not going to lie, but it feels good to have some *me* time for a few days.

Getting comfortable on my couch, I press *play* on my remote and my favorite show, *Suits,* comes on. Honestly, there's something about men in suits that makes me melt and go stupid. A well-tailored suit on a handsome man makes him *that* much sexier. Especially with a tie; definite panty dropper.

Twenty minutes into the episode I'm watching, the doorbell rings. I pause the show and walk to the door, hating whoever is ruining this moment.

"Girls night!" Lexi and Karly shout. They're holding bags of food and wine.

"Come on in." I smile, leading them in and shutting the door. "What made you want to come over?"

"Nicholas said that Jensen's out of town, so we thought it would be fun to get together. You know, see how you're doing and what's going on."

"Pretty much we wanna know what's up with you and Jensen," Lexi adds.

"Exactly." Karly gives me a smile and sits on the barstool at the island. I reach in the cabinets and grab three wine glasses. "So what's going on between you and Jensen?"

I pop the cork out of the wine bottle and pour everyone a glass. Taking a few sips of my wine, I look at Lexi and Karly and think about what I want to tell them. "We're dating. He's amazing and we're in love." Saying this aloud to my friends, I don't know, it feels so good.

"Love!" Karly shrieks. "What?"

"That's so sweet," Lexi says, tipping her glass of wine to me and taking a drink.

"I'm really happy. I didn't think I would be able to move on, but I am. He listens to me and pushes me. We help each other."

"Wait, then, who was that guy on your phone? Remember when we went to the cafe?"

My chest tightens. I've talked to Jensen about Brody and he listened. It was nice to talk about him and tell him about the love we shared. It's still hard thinking about his death. With the holidays around the corner, I'm not sure what to do. I'm supposed to go to Montana and be with Isaac and his parents. Part of me wants to go and the other part is completely shattered. Going back to the place that holds all of our memories, causing the aches in my body to explode. Wincing at the thought, I droop my shoulders when I look at Karly and Lexi. I take another step forward and tell my two best friends about Brody.

When I'm done talking, they're both crying and hugging me, holding me in their arms. I'm crying with them. My nose is runny and my throat is sore. I clear my throat and wipe my tears, looking at them again.

"But it's okay because Jensen found me and I found him. He makes me smile and, with him, I feel like I can take this next step. I don't feel guilty. This is what Brody would want and I think Brody would like Jensen."

Thinking about Jensen heightens my body and I lose my mind. But in a good way. "Okay, can we please stop being sad and watch *Suits*?"

"Yes!" Lexi says. We bring our plates and wine glasses to the living room and get comfortable. We get comfortable on the couch and soon a whole lot of sexiness comes on the TV.

* * * * *

Kisses all over my face. I know he's next to me, holding me in his arms, but I don't want to wake up yet.

"If you want to see your surprise, you need to wake up, beautiful." My eyes open and a smile comes on my face. "Go to your closet and get your present."

I leap out of bed and run to my closet. When I open the door, I find a large box in the middle of the floor. Grabbing it with both hands, I bring it back out, sit on the floor, and open it. Lifting the top of the box, I see there is a pair of black boots.

"Oh my gosh!" Jensen bought me knee-high Stuart Weitzman boots. "Are you serious?" I squeal and try on one of the boots. It zips up perfectly until I realize that the material stretches.

"Don't do that."

Instantly I feel fat. I've been doing really well with keeping up with my gym schedule and not eating a lot. I've been losing inches and I'm a little more toned, but my weight is still the same. I stand up, look in the mirror, and curse my 165 pound body.

"I don't know why you're upset. Babe, you're beautiful."

I spin around and glare at him. "Because I can't wear normal boots. The material has to stretch in order for me to wear something like this. Don't get me wrong. I love that you bought these for me and I appreciate it. Just wish I were skinny like Lexi and Karly. I mean they've had babies and are still a size two!"

"Fallyn…"

Vision of Hope

"Stop," is all I'm able to say. I take off the boots and put them back in the box. "I'm gonna shower." Closing the door, I turn on the water, strip out of my clothes, and break down, feeling the water on my body.

Pulling myself out of the shower, I wrap a towel around my body and walk back to the bedroom. Jensen's standing before me, wearing his boxer briefs, and he's staring at me.

"Jensen?" Without saying a word, he takes three long strides to me and kisses the tip of my nose.

"Fallyn, you're everything to me. I want you to be happy because your happiness means the world to me. I hope I didn't offend you."

I shake my head. "It's still hard."

"Close your eyes," he mumbles. I do as he says and feel his hands on my shoulders, guiding me a few feet to my right. I feel the towel fall from my body. I want to cover myself. The thought of Jensen staring at my naked body is making my stomach hurt and my heart want to leap out of my chest.

"Open your eyes," he says. When I open my eyes, I see him staring at me in the mirror. "Do you see what I see?"

"No." I shake my head.

"Well, I see the most beautiful woman before my eyes." His hands trace my collarbone, down my breasts, to my soft belly. "I don't care if your stomach isn't flat." His hands grip my hips and he pulls me back into him. "Do you feel me?" My breathing is erratic and I'm not able to answer.

"I need you to answer me," he says in my ear. Our eyes are still on one another. "Do. You. Feel. Me?"

"Yes," I croak.

"What do you feel?"

Trying to find my voice, and failing miserably, I close my eyes. Tipping my head back, I wrap my arms around his neck and bring it down to my neck so I can feel his lips on me.

186

Moving my head to the side, giving him enough space, he kisses the sensitive spot by my earlobe.

"I feel how hard you are. I'm making you hard."

"Yes." He kisses me again, dipping his hand down to my center. "And do you feel how wet you are for me?"

"Yes," I let out. "Touch me."

"I want you to say something."

"Anything."

He stops kissing my neck and grabs my chin so that I'm looking at myself in the mirror. "I want you to say *Fallyn, you are beautiful and have a sexy-ass body.*"

He sees my hesitation and grips my hips tighter, causing me to let out a little whimper. His grip isn't hurting me, but I know he needs me to say this.

I need to say this.

"Fallyn, you are beautiful and have a sexy-ass body."

I finally lean into his body and let him take control. "Put your hands on the mirror and don't take your eyes off me."

"Yes," I pant, wanting him, desiring for him to be inside me. "Please," I beg,

He plays with my clit and slides two fingers in me. I moan, placing my hand on top of his. I don't break eye contact. His eyes are hooded and full of desire. Shit, I'm about to come right now.

"I need you to fuck me," I order him. "I need to feel your hard cock in my pussy." I have no idea where these words are coming from, but staring at him while he pleasures me with his fingers brings out the animal in me.

"My pleasure," he smirks and enters me, filling me hard and quick.

His eyes stay on mine as he fucks me hard. It feels so good and so naughty. I love it. My boobs bounce from him entering me and pulling out. I don't care, though. This is turning him on and making him want me. Desire me.

Vision of Hope

This isn't a simple one-time fuck. This is a love fuck. We love each other and I do this to him. I make him hard and make him moan. The sexy noises coming from him are because of me. It's broad daylight and the sun shines in the room. He doesn't care that I jiggle or my body isn't tight. If he doesn't care, then I shouldn't either.

"Fallyn, come, baby," he shouts. "Fuck. Come, now."

And on command, I fall apart, and soon he does too. My whole body tenses and relaxes. Jensen picks me up and carries me to bed.

"Now that I've properly fucked you, I'm going to make sweet love to you. But first, I need to taste your delicious pussy and spend some time getting reacquainted with you."

"Oh God, Jensen."

* * * * *

Today, we're leaving for Montana and to say I'm nervous is an understatement. I check my suitcase for the millionth time to make sure I have everything. Then, I check Jensen's bag and zip both suitcases. Julie and Phil are excited to see us and Isaac's really proud of me for doing this.

"Hey, sis," Isaac says, coming into Jensen's room. I relax when I hear his voice and slide down to the bedroom floor.

"This is okay, right?"

"Yeah, it is. You're over thinking this. Brody would want to meet the man who is responsible for putting that smile on your face."

I haven't thought about Brody in days. "Sometimes, I feel like I'm forgetting him. Am I?"

Isaac shakes his head. "It means you're doing what he wants and you're moving on. We're proud of you."

I get up and give Isaac a hug. "Thank you for saying the things I need to hear."

"Always."

Isaac brings down the suitcases and we head down. Jensen's checking the house to make sure everything is turned off and we're ready to leave. Being away for one full week is necessary. Work has been up and down, so this vacation will be spent with us relaxing and forgetting about home for a little.

We gather our things and Jensen turns on the alarm system before we load up in Stephen's SUV.

"I wish you were coming too," I tell him.

"Well, me and my beautiful girlfriend are heading to New York City to be with her family," he announces. Ever since Stephen committed to Leslie, he's been on cloud nine. I still haven't met her and I'm so mad he's hiding her from us.

"Well, we'll be here for Christmas, so I expect to meet my best friend's girlfriend."

"Deal. She wants to meet everyone too."

"Wait; what about Lisa?" Isaac asks.

"She decided to spend it with Ian's family," Stephen quietly answers.

"Good for her," I say, leaning back in the seat and looking out the window. Maybe now, she can leave Jensen alone and the fear of her around will go away.

Since the day at Nicholas and Karly's party, I haven't been able to shake off what she said about maybe leaving Fisher to come back to Wilmington. I know that she'd be back during her breaks and summers, but to have her back full time scares me. I know I need to be secure in my relationship with Jensen and I am. Lisa pushes my buttons and it takes everything in me not to want to hurt her.

Jensen gently shakes my shoulder. "Ready to board?"

I look at the passengers lining up to board then, to my loving and beautiful boyfriend. "Ready."

Chapter 29
Jensen

Our flight is about to land and I can see the anxiety in Fallyn's eyes and her body. Her arms are crossed across her chest and she's been looking out the window for the past hour. I tried calming her down, but she keeps telling me to go to sleep and she'll be fine. I know this is a huge step for her and I can't begin to understand how she's feeling. I'll be here for her, whatever she needs, and I hope this trip will help her heal and not push her back.

I grab our bags from the overhead compartment and notice Isaac has his arm around Fallyn. He's whispering something to her and she nods to what he's saying. To say I'm not hurt would be a lie. I want to be the one she turns to when she's feeling down and scared.

"Baby, are you okay?"

She looks at me and gets up from her seat. "Yeah," she softly answers. "Just really nervous about this week. Thank you for coming along. I don't know if I could do this without you."

I kiss the tip of her nose and help her out. Isaac follows us and we walk through the airport to meet his parents. When we walk through the sliding doors, Fallyn lets go of my hand and runs to, I'm assuming, Julie and Phil.

"My parents," Isaac says. "Come on so I can introduce you."

We walk over and Isaac hugs his parents as well. "Mom and Dad, this is Jensen Toscano. Jensen, my parents, Julie and Phil Andrews."

"Hi, Jensen." Julie kisses my cheek and hugs me. "So nice to meet you."

I shake Phil's hand and he says the same.

"I'm sorry." Fallyn blushes. "I was so excited to see them. Thank you so much for getting us from the airport and insisting on having Jensen come."

"No problem, honey. Come on; let's go get some dinner."

Fallyn takes my hand again and my worries about this week go away slightly. Somewhere in the back of my mind, I have a feeling when we go back to the Andrews house, she might not be okay. I'm holding on to the hope her strength, the beautiful strength she has, will be stronger than her broken heart.

We get to dinner and are seated around the hibachi table. The conversation is full and I can't help but fall in love with Fallyn's smile. She looks happy. The simple touch from her made me happy to be here. At first, I didn't think it was a good idea. I didn't want Isaac's parents to think I was marking my claim or anything along those lines. I'm here because she wants me here. I'm here to help her with she needs.

"So, Jensen, tell us more about what you do."

"I don't want to bore you, Phil." They laugh and Fallyn chimes in.

"He's the medical director and has been making such amazing improvements to the hospital. He's great and brilliant."

Julie's eyes light up. "I'm so glad to hear that. Fallyn, I must say," she adds, "you look so happy."

"Yeah," Fallyn answers. "I am. I won't lie. It's hard being here, but I'm okay."

Vision of Hope

"This was Brody's favorite place to eat," Isaac tells me, "He'd come here at least twice a week."

"I'd love to hear more about him." Julie's and Phil's eyes are on me. Wide and full of surprise. "Fallyn has told me some, but I'd like to know more, if that's okay."

Julie wipes a tear from her cheek and slowly nods her head. "Brody," she says, "was a great man. He was always so curious. It's because of him we have a love for sushi and hibachi."

"When we first came here," Fallyn laughs, "Phil looked at the sashimi and poked it a few times. He asked the hibachi chef if he could cook the salmon."

We start laughing. Fallyn holds her stomach, falling over. "The chef looked at him in surprise, and Phil was one hundred percent serious."

"What the hell was I supposed to do with raw fish?" he says. "I like my food cooked, thank you very much."

"Brody always liked to try new things. He didn't have any fears," Fallyn explains. "I never had sushi until I came here with Brody. Now, I love it."

"Same here," I agree. "I could eat sushi every day."

I listen to a few more stories and look at Fallyn. She's trying so hard to stay strong and not break down. This is good for her. Listening and talking about him. I take her hand in mine and bring it to my lips, lightly kissing the top of her hand.

"What's that for?"

"Just letting you know I love you and I'm happy to be here with you."

"You're amazing."

"You are too, baby. I love you." I kiss her hand again.

"I love you too."

The dinner starts and goes off without any issues. The chef is entertaining and keeps the room alive. He tosses balls of

192

rice and sake bombs into our mouths. Phil's face is as red as a cherry and we're laughing, having fun.

After dinner, Julie insists on paying and gives me her *don't mess with me* mom look. I back down very fast.

The drive to their house is quick and soon we're walking through their quaint home. Fallyn's shoulders tense and her breathing is fast. She looks around the house and sees pictures of her past. There's one picture that catches my eye. It's of Brody and Fallyn in the park. She's laughing and on his back. I can tell the love between them was strong. Am I jealous? No. I understand Fallyn had a life before me and she's still in love with him. I'd never try to take that away from her.

"I need a minute," she whispers and walks outside. I watch her walk away and I want to chase after her. Before I do, Julie grabs my arm.

"Give her some time. Phil and I want to talk to you, if that's okay. I nod my head and follow them into the living room. We sit down and Isaac joins me too. "Before Fallyn goes upstairs to Brody's room, which I know she will, we want you to know that his things aren't in there. We cleaned out the room last month and donated his clothes. Now there's a bed and we've turned it into a guestroom. It was hard walking by his old room. Now," Julie sniffs, wiping her tears, "please don't think we're cruel and heartless. We'll miss our son for the rest of our lives, but this is what he'd want. Brody wouldn't want anyone to mourn over his death forever."

"I understand," I respond. "But how will Fallyn take it?"

"She's gonna be a mess, man. This trip means the world to us, to my parents, to see her smile and be herself. But we know she's going to be a mess and she might push you away. So if you can, be there for her and understand where she's coming from."

"Of course. Whatever you need, I'm here. I love Fallyn and I want to spend my life with her." Julie gasps, while Phil and

Isaac smile. I know that Fallyn and I haven't been together for long, but when you know, you know. The way her eyes meet mine, the way she makes me feel, I want to feel this way for the rest of my life. This is real love; a forever love with her, and I hope to make it a reality soon."

"I think you're what she's been looking for, Jensen. Thank you for making our girl happy," Phil says. "We were afraid she wouldn't ever find happiness again. When Brody died," he chokes a bit, "we all lost a piece of ourselves that night. It's been a very difficult road and, like Julie said, we'll miss him for the rest of our lives, but we know that our children are in good hands and we know Brody's with our Heavenly Father."

"Like I said, whatever you need, please don't hesitate to ask."

"Love her," Julie exclaims. "Cherish her, and make sure she knows how special she is."

"That's easy." I smile. "If you'll excuse me, I'm going to go check on her."

I walk out the front door and find Fallyn sitting on the porch chair. She doesn't look up when she hears me walking to her. I sit down and think about taking her hand, but wait. We sit in silence and it's okay.

"Brody and I would sit here when we were younger. I used to be afraid of the dark, so we'd sit out here and talk. When I got tired, he carried me to his room and slept on the floor. My parents would get so mad that I spent the night with him." She laughs. "I've loved Brody for most of my life. I remember everything about him, but when I'm with you, I feel like I'm forgetting him." She looks at me with tears in her eyes. "I don't want to forget him. I don't want to be without you."

"What makes you think I'd let you forget him?"

"I don't want you to think I'm crazy or something."

"No." I shake my head. "I want your past, your present, and your future. I want it all, Fallyn. A piece of me is afraid

I'm taking you away from this life, and I don't want that. I know that Julie, Phil, and Isaac are your life. I'm jealous that you turn to Isaac. I want to be the one who dries your tears. I want to be the one you turn to when you're feeling sad. Will you let me be the one?"

She takes my face in her hands, cupping it ever so softly, and kisses me. When our kiss releases, her eyes look deep into mine and tears slowly start to form. "I don't know what to say."

"Tell me what's in your heart." My hand rests on her chest, feeling her heart beating. Doesn't this woman know I would do anything for her? I'd do anything to keep that beautiful smile on her face and make sure nothing will ever hurt her.

"You. You are in my heart." Her hand rests on mine. "I know you love me and I know you want to make sure I'll be okay. You're part of the reason I'm okay. I'm so thankful for you. Even though I get sad, or seem distant, that doesn't mean you aren't on my mind. I think about you all the time." The words she's speaking cut through me. It's hard not to get emotional by the honesty of her words. "I love you. I love Brody. I love you both. But *you* have me."

"I know there's another but."

She nods her head. "There're some things I have to do, but that doesn't mean I'm leaving you. Until I do these last few things, then I'll be able to open myself up to you fully. I hope you can understand that."

"As long as we're together. Please don't leave me." The tightness in my chest makes it hard to breathe. I would fight for her every day if she left me. Without her, there's no me. She's everything and I'm going to love her harder with each passing day.

"I'll never leave you, Jensen. Never."

I toss and turn throughout the night. We're sleeping in the other guest bedroom, down the hall from Brody's old room;

Vision of Hope

well, now the second guest bedroom. I turn my head and watch Fallyn sleep. What she said to me weighs heavy on my mind. I know she won't leave me, but I wonder what she needs to do and why she won't let me do this with her.

I'm in a place I never thought Fallyn and I would be in. Her words about not leaving play in my head. I have to believe she won't leave and she'll find whatever it is she's looking to do.

Chapter 30
Fallyn

It's five in the morning and no one else is up yet. I gently kiss Jensen's cheek and carefully get out of bed. Tiptoeing to my suitcase, I kneel down and unzip my bag. Pulling out a small box full of letters I've written to Brody since he passed away, I clutch it to my chest and walk out of the bedroom to his. I want to read every single letter to him before the house wakes up. This is the only time I'm going to do this and I want to do this right. I want him to know how much I love him and I'll love him forever. I want him to know that I'm happy and I'm ready for the future with Jensen. I'm ready for it all. I'm not going to run away from him or his love. Our love is better than fear of the unknown because Jensen's the one I've been waiting for.

I take a breath and walk into Brody's old room. Opening the door, I drop the box of letters and look around the room. All of his things are gone. The room looks like the room I'm in with Jensen. I run to the closet, swinging the door open and see extra blankets, pillows, and towels. Turning to the dresser, I frantically open each drawer.

Empty!
Empty!
Empty!
Empty!

All of his things are gone! I feel the tears rushing from my eyes. They took away his things and threw them away...without me.

Vision of Hope

I slam my fist into the wall, over and over again. Strong arms soon wrap around my waist and pull me off the ground.

"Let me go! Let me go! *Now!*"

"Shhhh, baby. Shhhh." His voice is so close, but so far. I can't hear anything. I look around the room, hysterical and worried. Everything's gone.

"Fallyn!" Julie yells and I hear more footsteps. I push myself off Jensen and turn around.

"*YOU* did this. *YOU* took his things *without me*. How could you?" Julie tears up and Phil holds her hand. I look at Isaac. "You could have told me. You could have warned me about this!"

"We thought Jensen would have done this with you."

Jensen? My Jensen?

"Get out of my way," I hiss. Without looking back, I run downstairs, throw on a pair of sneakers, and run out of the house. I need to be with Brody. I need Brody.

Brody.

Brody.

Brody.

Brody.

I run hard and fast. I don't look back. There are cars zooming by. Some are slowing down to look at me, but I don't pay them any attention. I run up the hill, make a quick right, and reach my destination.

Passing by the tombstones, I run deeper into the cemetery until I reach his.

Brody Alexander Andrews
April 25, 1991-March 17, 2014
Beloved son, brother, nephew, grandson, friend, and fiancé.
May you spread your wings and soar to the Heavens. Fly with the Heavenly Angels and never stop flying.

"Brody," I sob. "Brody, please let me know you're still here." Silence. "I need you so badly right now. I thought I was strong and I could move on, but your parents… they cleaned out your room and I didn't get to say goodbye. I have all these letters to read to you, but I wanted to do it while sitting on your bedroom floor. You know, how we used to. I didn't want to read you the letters here at your grave. This holds bad memories, but at least in your room, I remember all the times we shared." Silence. "Brody," I cry again. "Please, I need you. I need you." Lying down next to his grave, I place my hand on the grass and close my eyes. "I need to feel you."

Being here next to him opens the wounds from that night. There's so much I want to say to him. There's so much I want him to know. I thought I was ready to move on and have a future with Jensen. I'm not sure what to do anymore. I feel so lost and scared.

Brody's old bedroom held so many memories. We were so happy and so in love. He was my best friend and the only boy I've ever loved. When I was ten, after a week of being friends, I told my mom that I was going to marry him. I was going to be Mrs. Brody Andrews. That day never came. I never got to have his last name.

"Do you remember when I would sleep over your house? My parents *hated* that I slept over, but they loved you. You'd sleep on the floor and I'd sleep on your bed. The bedroom door would be wide open and your mom walked by us so many times. I remember your hand holding mine and we'd stay like that for so long. You held my hand through so much and you kissed away my tears. I need you to please do that again." Silence.

The tears burn the back of my eyes, rushing from my eyes and down my cheeks. I don't wipe away the tears.

"Please come back," I whisper. "Tell me you're still here."

Vision of Hope

I lie motionless, not sure what else to do. I stroke the grass with my hand, back and forth, closing my eyes, pretending I'm brushing away Brody's shaggy hair from his beautiful eyes. The eyes of love and tenderness. The eyes I love and will love until the day I take my final breath.

Memories of happier times flood my mind. These memories remind me of our strong love. He was my world and I was his. We spent nearly every day together and said *I love you* every day. Minus the mini-breakup, our lives were perfect. We were nominated "most likely to get married" and "happiest couple" our senior year of high school. We studied together and pushed each other with everything we did. He was my rock. I was his rock. He was the one I turned to when I had a bad day and he vented to me whenever he needed to. He held my hand through the scary movies and laughed during the funny times. We had designated date nights and paid attention to each other and no one else. He was my world and I was his.

"Give me a sign that everything will be okay. Give me something. Give me anything."

Images of Brody go through my mind. But this time, he's standing over my grave, looking at me, crying and asking *why*. I'm looking at me, heartbroken and devastated. This isn't what I would want for him. I wouldn't want him to mourn over me and spend his waking moments crying over me. Everyone deserves a second chance to love and be happy again. The images in my head get stronger and I see someone taking his hand. He looks up and smiles, which causes me to smile. I don't know who is holding his hand and I don't care. Whoever is holding his hand, well, I love her.

"Fallyn." I open my eyes, lift my head, and see my Angel rushing to me. "Fallyn!" He falls to his knees and brings me in his strong arms. Arms I love. Arms I want. "I'm so sorry, baby. I'm so fucking sorry. I should have warned you and been there for you."

I can't find the words I need to tell him it's okay. My voice is gone.

"Are you okay? I love you. Please don't be mad at me. Please."

I cup his face with my hands. "I'm okay. I promise."

He holds me tighter as I wrap my arms around his neck. A calming peace comes over me. I'm unafraid of the future because my future is giving me back the reason to believe. He saved me.

"I'm not mad at you anymore. I wanted to sit in his room, around his things, and read my letters to him. His room holds so many good memories." Jensen looks at me with love in his eyes and reaches into his jacket pocket.

"I brought these for you." *My letters.* "Maybe you can go to another spot that means a lot to you. I can walk with you there and give you space, but I won't be too far away."

My heart nearly bursts out of my chest. How did I get so lucky?

"Follow me." I take his hand in mine and we walk out of the cemetery to another favorite place of mine and Brody.

Missoula is beautiful around this time. The weather is a little colder today, but when Jensen handed me a jacket he brought for me, I pulled it on and hugged it against my body.

The walk to the park isn't too far and it's nice to walk around town, taking in the sights again, remembering how easy things used to be.

"Just around the corner." We walk for a few more minutes before I see the bench.

Our bench.

"This is the part I need to do alone."

"Okay, baby. I'll be at the diner. So text me when you're done." He lightly kisses my lips and holds my hand before letting me go and letting me do this one more thing.

I sit on the bench and press my hand against the old wood. This bench, our bench, *the* bench we used to sit on and spend hours holding each other's hands, looking around, taking in what was around us. This was where we got back together after taking a break. This was where I forgave him and told him I loved him and would always love him.

I take out the first letter.

My dearest Brody, I'm packing up my things and leaving tomorrow. I'm starting my life in Wilmington with Isaac and I wish it were you. Laying you down to rest was one of the hardest things I've ever had to do. I cried and begged God to bring you back to me, but he needed you in Heaven. I know you're up there now, smiling, but I wish you were here with me. How am I going to get through the rest of my life without you? You're my world and I'm so lost. Will you help guide me in the right direction?

I still hear your voice in my head. I still hear the last words out of your mouth. I can't move on and be happy. How do you expect me to do that?

You're the only man I've ever loved. You're the only man I've given my heart to and now you want me to move on? I'm not heartless. I can't and won't find happiness with anyone else. I think about taking my own life just so that we can be together again.

Please don't leave me. I still need you and will always need you.

I love you always and forever,
Fallyn.

I read the next few letters and keep the tears at bay. I know it sounds crazy, but I feel like he is sitting next to me. His presence is so strong.

My dearest Brody,
Today, I met someone. His name's Jensen Toscano and I think I might like him. We're spending more time together, and he's really sweet. He listens to me and I listen to him.
Things are going pretty well. I have our picture on my nightstand and look at it every night and every morning. You're still a part of me and I'm not letting you go.
It's getting easier to breathe. Is this because of you?
Please come visit anytime and let me know when you do.
I love you always and forever,
Fallyn.

The wind whooshes by, slight chills running over my face. More words and more letters until I reach the last one. The hardest letter.

My dearest Brody,
Tomorrow, I'm leaving to go back home and visit your parents. I'll be back in our hometown, the town we met in and fell in love. I'm scared to go back because it's been so long since I've been here to visit. It's been so long since I've visited your grave. I know you came to visit me a few minutes ago when I was outside on the deck. I felt your hand brushing my shoulder. Thank you for coming to see me.
I think about you every day, but Brody, I'm in love. I fell in love with Jensen and I'm so happy. Did you send him to me?
I think I'm going to tell him I'm fully ready to move on with my life. Oh, Brody, he's so sweet and understanding. He gets how much I still love you and wants to know more about you. We're going to keep your memory alive and I'll never forget

you. I'll never forget our love and what you mean to me. You will always have my love and my heart, Brody. Forever. Always and forever.

Until the day we meet again, please keep soaring above the clouds. Watch over me, Jensen, Isaac, and your parents.

I will miss you and love you for the rest of my life. Wait for me by Heaven's Gate and lead me in when it's my time.

I love you always and forever,

Fallyn.

Chapter 31
Jensen

"Please come back and visit us often." Julie kisses my cheek and turns to Fallyn and Isaac.

Phil shakes my hand and smiles. "Thank you for loving her and being there for her, Jensen."

"It's my pleasure. Thank you for accepting me into your lives and being the family she loves."

"She's our little girl," Phil says, looking adoringly at his wife and kids. "She's our world and you are too."

My heart clenches. The Andrews' were amazing this week and once Fallyn said and did what she needed to do, the weight and guilt of Brody's death lifted from her shoulders. She's smiling more and is happier. She found her way back to me and, as soon as we land, we'll be taking a next step into our future.

* * * * *

The next few days pass and Fallyn's been running around, getting things ready for Christmas. Both of our houses are decorated, but I've been noticing more of her things are finding a place in my home. Or should I say *our* home. I hope. When she's here, it feels like my home and life are whole. When she's not here, I'm sitting alone in a house full of silence. It's not fun and I find myself either at her house or somewhere else. I know that we haven't been together for long, but these feelings and my love for her are real and true. I

Vision of Hope

want to settle down and start my life. And I want to start it with her.

After I pour her a glass of crisp white wine, I settle back on the couch with her, resting my arm over her shoulders and feeling her weight of her head on my chest.

"Perfect," she sighs, staring at the six-foot tree we *had* to get.

I kiss the top of her head. "I'd like to give you your first present now if that's okay."

She perks up with wide eyes and a big smile on her face. "Yes!"

Pulling out a small box from my pocket, I hand it to her. "Open it."

In a matter of seconds, the wrapping paper is off, on the ground, and the box is open. "Are you asking me to move in?"

Shyly, I answer, "I am."

Fallyn gets up from the couch and goes into the kitchen. I peek over and glance at her movements, realizing she's picking up her keys and placing my house key with hers. "Now it's official." She skips over to me and goes back to her original position. "I love you."

"I love you more."

As I stroke her arm, we sit in silence, taking in the ambiance of the living room filled with Christmas joy. Her hand rubs my upper thigh and she giggles. In seconds, our clothes are off and she's straddling me. My mouth wraps around her nipples, sucking and biting, hearing her moan my name, wanting more.

She slides her tongue from the bottom of my lip, down my neck. Lifting up her hips, she takes my cock in her hand and slides down. "Fuck, you're so wet," I hiss, watching her ride my cock. Our eyes are on one another before I claim her mouth with my own. All I want is to feel her forever.

I grip her hips, feeling her muscles clench around me. I know she's close. Standing up, I push her against the wall, holding her ass in my hands, devouring her mouth. Her nails dig into my back when I pump harder into her. I pump deeper and she bites down on my shoulder. This pain, the fucking good pain, pushes me over the edge and I slam into her tight pussy harder.

"Yes!" she screams as we find our release together. When I set her down, she feathers my face with kisses. There's a glow on her face as she takes my hand and leads me upstairs.

"I want you to make love to me now," she seductively whispers. "Nice and slow."

"Oh yes," I mutter, taking her lips, savoring her kiss, nice and slow.

We wake the next morning, together, and get ready for work. It's a day full of meetings and Fallyn's expecting three more patients in her wing. She's been working days with some nights since we've been back. I don't want her working the overnight shifts, and she understands. I know it's hard for her to be away from her patients, but as medical care providers, we too need rest before tackling another day.

Driving through traffic, Fallyn's playing with the radio and then her phone. "Karly wants us to come over tonight. She said to bring ice cream."

"Sounds good, love."

Parking my car in my spot, I open the door for Fallyn and we walk together, hand in hand. Giving her a quick kiss, I tell her to have a good day and go inside my office. There's a package waiting for me when I sit down. Not checking who it could be from, I open the card and immediately know who it's from.

Jensen,

Vision of Hope

Saw this and thought of you. I miss you like crazy. Please talk to me.

Love,

Lisa

I open the box and see a New York City key chain with a few other knickknacks. We had plans to go to the city over New Year's, but plans change and so does life.

Picking up my phone, I think about texting her. I'm not sure what I'd say besides thank you. Pulling up her contact information, I look at it and lean back in my chair. If it's this hard to text her, then it's not a good idea. I put away my phone and start my day with emails and returning phone calls.

The strangest feeling comes over me. I'm not sure what exactly it is, but I feel like someone's watching me. I take out my phone again and text Fallyn.

Me: *Are you okay?*

Fallyn: *Yeah. Why?*

Me: *I don't know. The weirdest feeling hit me...Like someone's watching me or something...Just wanted to make sure you're okay.*

Fallyn: *Just dandy =) I gotta go and check on some patients...Don't worry so much...I love you XOXOX.*

Me: *I love you too.*

As long as she's okay, then it's probably in my head. I get through the rest of the day without worrying until she's standing in my office waiting for me.

"Why are you smiling?"

She locks the door and turns off the light. I kink my brow at her and lean back in my chair, watching the way she slowly walks to me. Placing her hands on my thighs, she kisses my lips ever so lightly. "I have a surprise for you."

"Okay. Show me then."

Walking over to where she's placed her purse, she pulls out a bag and my eyes are looking, wondering what she's holding in her hands. "I didn't want to wait until we were home to use this and I've always had a fantasy about office sex." Her tone is seductive and my cock is hard as a fucking rock, straining against my pants. "I went to the store on my lunch break in case you were wondering why we didn't see each other." Fallyn pulls her bun out and her hair splays down her shoulders – today, it's wavy, and beautiful – while she stands in front of me. Pulling off her shirt and pants, she's standing in front of me, wearing a very revealing and sexy black corset with red lace. My eyes roam her body and I lick my lips, looking at her long legs.

"Turn around for me."

She does and the sight of her ass in a black lace thong nearly makes me explode. She's beyond fucking sexy.

Before I can say anything else, she comes to me and rubs her ass on my cock. Her hands caress my thighs as she moves up and down. My own personal lap dance.

"Do you like me dancing for you like this?" She turns around, straddling me, and brings my face into her boobs. Goddamn.

"Oh fuck, baby." I rock my erection into her center and, in seconds, our clothes are off and I have her bent over my table, ramming into her from behind. I reach around and play with her clit.

"Oh God, Jensen. Yes! Yes! Please fuck me harder."

Removing my hand from her clit, I grab her hips and move faster and harder. She keeps calling out my name and I pray to God no one can hear what's going on in my office. Her pussy muscles are tight around my cock.

"Come!" I growl, releasing myself in her. I collapse, bringing her down with me, and hold her against my body. "Damn, baby."

"Yeah, that was pretty hot."

"Did I make your fantasy a reality?" Fallyn nods, kissing my neck and chest.

"Oh, you sure did. Every time we have sex, I swear to God, it gets better and better. I love how you're spontaneous and adventurous. What made you want to do this?"

Fallyn lets out a laugh and rests on her forearms. "Because with you, I feel like I can do these things and know you love it. You make me feel sexy and I love knowing how I can make you feel. I love making love with you. I love fucking you. I love everything we do together because it means so much more than just sex." I look into her blue eyes, realizing how much I love her and want to spend my life with her. The cutest smile comes on her face and she makes me smile back at her.

"I don't know how you can look so fucking cute after the way we just fucked like that."

"It's a talent and it's because of you."

I get up and help her as well. "Let's go home so we can have a part two and three."

"What about Karly's?" She giggles, taking out her phone. "We can't ditch them!"

"Yes," I nod, "Yes we can."

We put our clothes back on and head out of my office. I never thought loving someone as much as I love Fallyn would happen to me. I would die for her. I would do anything for her.

The vibration of my phone on the nightstand wakes me up. Carefully, I move, not waking Fallyn, and see a call from Lisa. It's past two in the morning.

"Lisa?" I whisper. "Why are you calling so late?"

I hear her sniffling and moving around. "I did something stupid. But all I wanted was to get you back and now I know that it'll never happen."

"What are you talking about?" I get up and swiftly move out of the room. "What did you do?"

"You were the one for me and I messed up. I thought that we could get back together and start over. I didn't think I would lose you and I did. I thought I was going to be okay, but seeing how happy you are with Fallyn breaks my heart. It makes me realize how stupid I was for letting you go." She sobs on the phone. "I love you, Jensen, and I'll always love you. But don't worry; I won't be bothering you anymore."

"Lisa. Lisa!" She doesn't answer, but the call is still active. I turn to head back to my room and see Fallyn sitting on the bed. Before I can say anything, she grabs my jacket and hands me my keys.

"Go to her. She needs you."

"But...."

"It's okay." She leans up and kisses my lips. "It's okay."

Chapter 32
Lisa

There's beeping around me. I slowly open my eyes and see Jensen sitting beside me. He's on his phone, but I can't read his expression. Quietly moving my eyes around the room, I notice that I'm in a hospital.

"Jensen."

"You're up. How are you feeling?"

I try to move my head to the side to face him, but everything hurts. My head is throbbing and my mouth is dry. "I feel like shit. What happened?"

"Honestly, you don't remember?" His voice is soft, but heavy with anger. Moving closer to my head, he glares at me. "You called me. I went to your house and saw you passed out with an empty bottle of pills, so I rushed you to the hospital. They had to pump your stomach and you've been out since you've been here."

The memories of the pills and vodka come to me. Remembering wanting to take my own life because being here without Jensen isn't the life I want. "Please listen to me."

"No." He shakes his head. "Lisa, what you did wasn't right. Stephen's a mess and he should be here soon. Everyone's worried about you. If I didn't get to you in time, then we wouldn't be having this conversation."

"I want you to believe me, Jensen. I don't know why I did that. I wanted you to give me one more chance."

"This isn't how you get my attention, Lisa. Come on; you're smarter than that. Why'd you do it?"

The sobs escape my lips and I close my eyes, not wanting to see his face. Shaking my head, I cry harder, unable to catch my breath. "I want you back. Please come back to me. Please. I'm so miserable without you."

Jensen takes my hand in his. "Lisa, you're always gonna mean something to me, but I've moved on. I'm starting my life with Fallyn and I'm happy. I know this is hard for you to understand, but I am happy and I want the same for you. You're with Ian. Be with him."

"No," she cries, "No. Ian isn't you. Every day that we're apart makes me realize how stupid I was to let you go. I mean how can she make you happy?"

"She just does."

"So where does this leave us?"

He sighs and let's go of my hand. I still can't bear to look at him. "Friends. That's all I can give you."

How am I supposed to understand this and only look at him like a friend? "I need time alone, Jensen." Before he can say anything, Stephen comes in and the look on his face nearly takes my breath away. He's so upset. His eyes are bloodshot and his face is pale.

Jensen leaves and gives Stephen a hug before walking out of the room. I cry and my cries turn into sobs. Images of pills and alcohol come to my head. I don't want to be alive! I hate feeling broken and lost. I need Jensen, and if he won't come back to me, then I don't want to be alive.

"Jensen!" I scream, trying to take off the wires from my arms. "Jensen!"

"Lisa," Stephen says, taking my hand. "Why? Why would you do this? Please stop." He holds my shoulders and makes me look at him. "Stop! Please, just stop. I need you to talk to me."

"I don't want to be alive," I sob. "I want him back! Jensen," I scream, pushing Stephen away.

Vision of Hope

"You need to calm down, please, and talk to me."

"I can't."

"Why?"

"Because I'm so miserable without Jensen. My biggest regret just walked out the door, Stephen. I know that I'm being selfish and I know that I made a big mistake, but he needs to forgive me. I need him to forgive me. I used to make him smile like that."

He pushes the hair from my face and rubs my hand. "I know that it hurts and I know you want so much more, but taking your life isn't the answer. You need to rise above this. You're with Ian now. You've been spending time with him and his family so don't make the same mistake twice."

I take in his words, and nothing is registering. "I need time alone, please."

"Okay," Stephen tells me. "I'll be in the waiting room." He leans down and kisses my forehead. "I love you, Lisa."

"You too."

The moment the door closes, I lean against the pillow and press my nails against my skin. The pain I'm inflicting on myself doesn't measure to the pain in my heart. I need to release the fucking pain. I need to find the release. I can't live like this.

I press harder, biting my lip so I don't scream, but it's not doing what I need it to do. Making a fist, I punch myself in the face, over and over again. The screams become loud and I hit myself until I feel arms around me.

There are voices around me. Everything is hushed and I don't know who's around me and who's talking. The garbled voices piss me off. Why are people in my room? Why won't they leave me alone?

A sharp pain is in my arm and, in seconds, I'm closing my eyes and feel light. The last thing I see is Jensen.

Jensen.

I'm not sure how many days pass. Have days passed or just hours? My mind is reeling, but the voices are still strong and loud. The internal struggle of facing reality hits me and I force myself to wake up. Trying to move my arms to itch my face is impossible.

What the hell is going on?

Waking up with restraints around my wrists is not how I want to wake up. Why is this happening? Why does my face hurt?

"Lisa?" I look up and see Stephen in the chair beside me. In the corner, Lexi, Karly, and Jensen are standing, looking at me, and judging me.

"I want everyone to leave!" I scream. "Get the fuck out! None of you were there for me when I needed you and now that I'm locked in this fucking hellhole, you want to be with me. No! Get out!"

"Calm down, Lisa." Jensen says, walking to me, placing his hand in mine. "We're here for you."

"Lisa, we're here for you," Lexi says and Karly agrees.

No. "I don't want any of you here, so leave now."

Anger and frustration course through me. The rush of feeling alone sinks in. As much as I want Jensen and my friends near me, I can't lie here and have them watch me at my lowest. No.

"If you need anything, please let us know." Karly kisses my forehead and walks out with Lexi and Jensen.

"Why'd you do that?"

"Because I can. I told you I want to be alone."

The shadows of self-doubt and loathing comes to surface, not hiding away from me. The voices in my head get louder.

No one wants you.

Go kill yourself.

You're nothing.

No one loves you.

Vision of Hope

I move my head from side to side. "Be quiet! Stop talking! Stop!" Stephen presses a button and people rush in. "No! Stop! Get away!"

* * * * *

The next few days are hard and Stephen's been taking care of me. Leslie, his girlfriend, is living with him now and they're helping me, but I don't want it. I want to be alone. I've been prescribed medication and I take it as directed, under the supervision of Stephen and Leslie. I'm an adult, but a child, locked away in my room, away from society.

It's my choice, though, to stay in my room. People have been coming to visit me and my phone is beeping with messages. I ignore it all. I'm slowly slipping away. There's no one to hang on to, no one to ask for help, no one who cares. My shoulders drop and I pick up the letter I've been writing to Jensen.

Jensen,

Throughout my life, I've never really had love until you. I made a mistake and now I have to live with that for the rest of my life. The regret I feel is so strong, but I know you're happy and as much as it hurts to say this, I think I'll be okay.

You've taught me so much about life and being strong. Well, it's my turn to stand on my own two feet and get the help I need.

Thank you for giving me the love I've always wanted. Thank you for showing me what it's like to feel love and wanted.

I wish you and Fallyn a life full of happiness.

I'm not sure how to end the letter, but the weight of regret lifts from my chest. I breathe in and out, putting the letter away, deciding it's best to finish it later.

My bedroom door opens and Leslie comes in. "Are you up for any visitors?"

"Sure."

Ian comes in and he's carrying flowers and a teddy bear. "Hi."

Leslie leaves the room and Ian comes over to me, keeping his space, and sits down. He hands me my gifts and our eyes don't move from one another. "Hi," I finally let out. "What are you doing here?"

"Your brother told me. I've been trying to reach you and, when I couldn't, I called him and he told me what happened." Ian hangs his head. "Why didn't you come and talk to me? I would have been here for you."

"I don't know. I mean, I told you I didn't want to be with you and left you. I didn't think you'd want anything to do with me."

"How could you think that?" Ian moves closer, cupping my face with his hands. "I know what we did was bad, but I think about you all the time. I love you, Lisa. I love you so much and I want you to be mine. I know that you're hurting now and I'll wait for you. Like I said before, I will wait. I'll be here whenever you need someone."

"How can you want to be with me? I'm a mess." My chest is heavy. His features are soft and warm. The seriousness in his tone is pushing me back; I am not sure how to feel. My eyes quickly shut and I count in my head.

"I get it." I'm looking at Ian, who is sitting in front of me, pouring out his heart, telling me he wants to be with me regardless of what I did or how I feel. Reaching deep in my heart, thinking about the times we've spent together, the idea

Vision of Hope

of being with Ian is comforting. But I have to let go of the past and love myself.

"I need time. I'm entering myself into a rehab. I'm not doing well, Ian."

He kisses my forehead. "Whatever you need, Lisa. I'm going to be here, waiting for you. When you change your mind, I'll be here. I love you." He kisses my lips and pulls me in his arms.

* * * * *

Holding the tickets in my hands, I turn back and look at Stephen and Leslie. I'm going to do this. For the first time in my life, I'm realizing my problems and issues. In order for me to get better and get my life back on track, I need to get the help I need, and being here in Wilmington or back in Rochester won't help me.

"Are you going to be okay?"

I nod. "Yeah, I think I am. Can you give this to Jensen, please?"

Stephen eyes me and I hand him the letter. I watch him put the letter in his inside jacket. Leslie and I hug and she wishes me luck.

When Stephen hugs me, I do everything I can to hold in my tears. "Thank you for being the best big brother. I love you."

"Take care of yourself. Okay?" I nod. Giving them final hugs, I head towards security and, finally, I can breathe.

* * * * *

It's been sixty-seven days since I've been in this facility. Everyone is really nice and supportive. I love my therapist and how real he is.

"How are you feeling today, Lisa?"

"Better," I answer. "So much better. It's been almost twenty days and I haven't thought about killing myself. I *want* to get better, Jack." Jack. My therapist. He's not like the other ones. We sit on the floor in his office and talk. Sometimes we talk about what's on TV or the music on the radio. He doesn't push me, but guides me to understand. I like Jack.

"That's great. I like that you're writing entries in your journal. You're getting there." He lifts his hand in the air and I give him a high five.

"I am getting there."

After the session, I head back to my room and see a stack of letters on my desk. I flip through each one, but see two that catch my eye. I open the first one.

Lisa,

I wrote this letter a few times, but I think I figured out what I want to say to you. I'm glad you're getting the help you need and I'm glad I got to you in time. You're a great woman and you have a lot to offer.

Our love was great and, yes, we made mistakes, but that's part of life. I know you're going to be okay and I'll be here for you, whatever you need. You're strong, keep telling yourself that.

Fallyn and I are doing well. Thank you for wishing us well.

I hope we see you soon. Take care of yourself.

-Jensen

I hold the letter to my chest and feel good. I don't cry. There's no reason to cry. I open the second letter.

Vision of Hope

To the girl who has my heart,

I think about you all the time. Stephen tells me you're doing well, but still won't have visitors and that's okay. I'm still waiting for you. I'm always going to wait for you.

I hope you can find it in your heart to let me in and let me love you. I know we left things unclear, but I promise you I'm here. Always here.

I haven't given up on us, Lisa. I'll never give up. I love you. Yours forever,

Ian

I'm going to be okay.

Chapter 33
Fallyn

Six months later…

"Larry, do you mind?" Jensen yells, pushing him away from me, making him fall in the pool.

I lift myself up from the pool chair, removing my sunglasses, and die laughing. Karly jumps up from her chair, gets on Jensen's back, and tries to get him in. He doesn't budge until we're all on him and fall in.

Larry grabs me by the waist and tosses me over his shoulder like a caveman. "Look what I have in my arms," he taunts Jensen. "Dude, your fiancée is so hot."

Lexi and Karly whoop and Jensen looks like he's ready to kill Larry. I smile when the word "fiancée" is said. I'll never get tired of hearing it. My heart races, thinking about our wedding day and saying "I do."

Jensen and I have been engaged for three weeks and I love every minute. We've had a wild ride, from accepting Brody's death to Lisa's suicide attempt and his help to accept myself for who I am. This journey that we've been on and continue to travel won't end anytime soon.

Looking over to the side, I see Lisa holding her stomach with Ian next to her. We smile at one another and I turn back to look at Jensen, the man who loves me with every piece of his soul.

We're having a small wedding with close friends and family in a few weeks. I don't care that I'm not going to have a flashy wedding. I found my Prince Charming and he's giving

Vision of Hope

me the fairytale wedding I want. The dress has been picked out and everything is near complete. We've been waiting for this day for so long and soon it'll be here.

"Give. Me. Back. My. Girl," he seethes and Larry hands me over to him without argument. "Why do you wear the smallest bikinis? Can't you wear pants and a sweater?" I playfully hit his chest and give him a kiss.

"It's summer, babe. And I'm having fun enjoying the sun with everyone. Plus, I have abs!" I point at my stomach and he shakes his head, smiling.

"As soon as the priest announces us as Mr. and Mrs. Jensen Toscano, I'm taking you to our room and we're going to practice making babies."

A family with Jensen.

"That sounds like a plan, my soon-to-be husband."

I look down at my three-stone diamond engagement ring, loving how it feels on my finger. When I look at the ring, I smile, not only because I have an amazing man in my life, but I have the strength to be happy.

There are still a lot of times I get quiet and sad, thinking about Brody and hoping he's happy with me. I know he wants me to be happy and that's all I need to know to push away the dark thoughts.

The night Jensen put the ring on my finger, everything became clear. We were at dinner with Julie, Phil, and Isaac, about ready to leave when he took my hand and told me how I've changed his world and, with me, he's a better man. As soon as he got down on one knee, I got up from my chair, jumped in his arms, and said *yes* over and over again.

Julie and Phil cried while Isaac hugged us both. I felt someone else touching my hand and knew it was Brody. He was giving us the *okay* and even though I didn't see him or hear his words, feeling his touch was all I needed.

Jensen is exactly what I need in this crazy world. I'll always be sad and feel myself falling back, but I know Jensen is going to be there to help pull me out. He's the anchor I've been looking for, keeping me down and grounded.

"Come on, you guys! Time to eat!" Nicholas yells and we get out of the pool to sit at the table.

Karly and Nicholas get their kids, Emma and Sebastian, ready while Larry and Lexi get Kayden and seat him in between the two. Isaac sits down with his new girlfriend, Elissa, and Stephen helps his pregnant wife, Leslie, down. Lisa and Ian join us at the table and we're all together.

"A toast," Jensen says, raising his beer in the air. We all follow suit. "Family. We aren't friends. We're family. We're each other's rocks and shoulders when needed. We'll be there for one another through thick and thin. The problems we've all experienced together have brought us here today. To family."

"To family," we repeat and clink our drinks with one another.

Family.

The family I've always wanted and needed. I look around at the table and smile. Sure, some of us didn't start on the right foot, but look at us now. It doesn't matter how you start as friends as long as, one day, you're able to look at them and accept them in your life. In life, you're going to experience the good, the bad, and the ugly. Sometimes, you'll fall and, sometimes, you'll be strong enough to fight through. It's okay to ask for help and it's okay to fall as long as you're able to get yourself up.

"What are you thinking about?" he whispers in my ear, touching my thigh.

"You," I tell him. "Who would have thought we'd be here today?"

"Life's funny like that. You came into my life when I needed you and you helped me realize the true meaning of love." He kisses the tip of my nose and takes my hand. "I love you."

"I love you too."

The overwhelming feeling of love from Jensen, pouring his heart to me, never letting me forget his love, is more than I deserve. I didn't feel alone anymore. I don't feel like I am lost. Leaning my head on his shoulder, I feel a breeze through my hair. Lifting my head, I slowly turn and see my parents, sister, and Brody smiling at me.

We love you so much, Fallyn. No matter where you are, we'll be right by your side, sweetheart. Always, we love you and we're so proud.

We love you.

S. Moose

Be sure to sign up below for my newsletter!
You'll receive monthly exclusive news, giveaways, sneak peeks and many more!

Your information will not be shared.

http://eepurl.com/2Gm5b

Reading reviews is one of my favorite things to do! I love reading your thoughts! Please be sure to leave your review on the retailer's site you purchased *Vision of Hope* from. Your constructive reviews truly help me grow. Thank you so much for letting my words into your mind and heart.

XOXOXOXO

Acknowledgements

First, thank you to my amazing readers, for believing in me and supporting me. Being an author is the best job and I love connecting with you and hearing how my books made you feel. This wouldn't be possible without you.

Thank you to my family and friends for your constant support. I don't know where I'd be without your love.

Sandi, thank you for always being there whenever I need you. You mean so much to me and I'm so thankful to have you as my mentor, critique partner, and best friend.

Kaylee, thank you for helping me write and plot this book. I truly appreciate you taking the time to sit and read this story and give me your honest thoughts. You're an incredible friend.

Lexi, I know I tell you this all the time, but thank you for being my PA and friend. You're always there when I need you.

Beth, you're a wonderful editor and friend. Thank you for calming me down and being the eyes I need.

Golden, thank you for your talent and friendship. You make these shoots so fun! It means so much to see my vision come to life and it's thanks to you. Tackle hugs!

Kelsey, thank you for my beautiful cover! Your work is incredible.

To my amazing BETAs, when you take the time, away from your family, to help me, there are no words to every tell you how much that means to me. Thank you for staying by my side and your support.

To Ena and Jennifer with Enticing Journey, thank you so much for all that you do. The both of you are so important to me.

To my PR company, Eye Candy Bookstore, thank you for your hard work and support. A special thanks to Kellie Montgomery for always staying on top of everything.

To my author friends, thank you for everything. I appreciate the shares and love. You make this community better and it means the world to me to have you in my life.

To the bloggers, I don't know where to start. You're all so amazing and I wish I could meet you all one day. Thank you for taking the time to help me promote my work. You're so vital and I hope you know that.

To my babes, thank you for sharing my work and letting me always vent to you. To the moon and back!

Finally, thank you to Ryan Patrick. You amaze me every day. I am so proud of you and thankful that you came into my life. You mean so much to me and you're my best friend. Thank you for your love and support.

About the Author

S. Moose is a *New York Times* and *USA Today* Bestselling author, living in Webster, NY with her family, friends, and shorkie, Charlie.

A 2011 St. John Fisher graduate, S.Moose loves to read and write. She enjoys getting lost in the fictional world and creating a place where readers can fall in love and swoon over the cute boys she brings to life.

When she isn't in her room in front of her computer or a book, she is with her family and friends being silly and enjoying life. She's romantic at heart and loves anything with a happily ever after.

Vision of Hope

S. Moose loves connecting with her readers! Be sure to visit her at:

Web: smoosewrites.blogspot.com
Email: smoose0609@yahoo.com
Facebook: www.facebook.com/S.Mooseauthor
Twitter: @S_Moose060912
Instagram: instagram.com/s_moose0609

Made in the USA
Middletown, DE
25 April 2015